So What?!

A Novel

By: Kym Chappell

This is a work of fiction. Names, characters, organizations, places, and incidents are either products of the authors imagination or used fictitiously.

©2018

ISBN-9780692168226

For Monique....

Gone but never forgotten

Introduction

They say the minute you stop looking for the one, he shows up. Well friends, this isn't that kind of story. This is not going to be a tale of love lost and love found again. This is a story about fuck ups, make ups, laughs, and lessons learned along the way.

Friendship is a beautiful thing but doesn't come without bumps and bruises. Things fall apart, feelings get hurt, and stupid shit happens, but so what?

Hold on to your seats, this is going to be a bumpy ride. Life is short! So, laugh, cry, cuss, be silent, be kind, be brave...but no matter what you do, enjoy life, because you only get one!

Chapter 1

Where my girls at?

Who runs the world? Girls! Who runs the world? Girls!

The song blasts throughout the nightclub as the lights are flashing, drinks are flowing, the dance floor completely packed with people. Kylisha DeBrow and her four girlfriends are at the corner table of the plush pink and black colored VIP section, each with a champagne glass in the air, singing and dancing to the song like its Friday night and they do not have to be up for work in the morning.

Kylisha raises her glass once more and yells, "Cheers to the freaking weekend!" followed by, "Okay, I know it's not the weekend yet, but I had to make a good RiRi reference. I love her!"

"Whose idea was it to have a celebratory outing on a Thursday, again?" Kylisha thinks to herself, oh yeah, it was mine. This is going to hurt in the morning. But so what? #girlsnightout is in full effect!"

"Ooh girl that is my jam!" Tangi says, throwing her hands up and starts dancing as the DJ mixes the next song in. The ladies laugh. Every song has been her jam all night. Known as Tan for short, Tangi Charles puts the curve in curvaceous, stands at approximately 5'5" with long faux goddess locks, has beautiful mocha skin and a beautiful smile. She is one of those women who are naturally beautiful and has a sense of style that is out of this world, even in what she calls a simple last minute outfit for tonight's outing- a white graphic t-shirt, black leather skirt, red belt, and electric yellow Louboutin pumps. She looks stunning and all eyes are on her.

Tangi graduated from The Fashion Institute of Technology and got her first job as a stylist for a morning talk show in New York. Although her dream was to always be a designer, she figured styling would be a good stepping stone. She then moved on to and continues to style for several television shows, alongside becoming a stylist for a selection of

New York's socialites, from assisting for special events to planning travel outfits, and closet organization for each season – a fashionista's dream. Now that she lives in Los Angeles, she's been doing more styling for television, she still has some high-profile clients she styles for, but her true focus at the moment is starting her own line. To her friends, Tan is always ready to party and is so much fun, but will drive you crazy with her "everything should be a yes because I'm your friend" attitude. She just loves having "yes" men and women in her life, which goes without saying has caused her to have some serious conflicts with her friends.

In a cute Dolce & Gabbana floral midi dress, lime green strappy Gucci heels, holding her drink in one hand and a water bottle in the other, is Leslie McCall. She's tall, thin, toned to the max, and has legs for days. Her beautiful long jet black hair is in a sleek low ponytail with a middle parting for tonight. Leslie has dark chocolate brown skin, big pretty round eyes, full lips, and super high cheekbones. She also has what the ladies call the Cindy Crawford mole on the right side of her upper lip that polishes off her supermodel physique/persona.

She is known as the level-headed friend, but has also been caught for sometimes riding the fence, mostly because she doesn't want to hurt anyone or appear like she is taking sides, How ironic is that? Considering she's a corporate attorney. Leslie is married to Mike McCall, they met her senior year of undergrad, followed each other to law school and now run one of the largest law firms in Los Angeles.

Smiling from ear to ear as the DJ whips up another mix is the newly made partner of one of LA's most prestigious sport management firms, Evian Graham. If you're a star athlete, 9 times out of 10, Evian represents you. Better known as E, the ladies call her their sister from another misses and mister. Evian has deep green eyes, pretty chestnut brown hair with blonde highlights, and porcelain white skin. She's about 5'8" and has a smile that literally lights up any room she steps into. Still in her work outfit, a black Calvin Klein sheath dress with nude Kate Spade pumps, she moves her beautiful hourglass figure to each beat of the music, fully living in the moment.

The girls call her the Momma Bear of the group, as she is always motivating and always pushing them to do their best, even when they don't want her to. No one wants you to be great as much as Evian. She is the one who pushed Kylisha into starting her own fashion magazine, now one of the biggest in the industry, making her name the Oprah of the fashion publishing world. Evian also is the one who told both Mike and Leslie that running their own firm was the way to go.

Laughing and pointing at Tangi's dancing craze is Asia. Asia is petite 5'3", with a very toned and muscular body to die for. Her signature long bob cut literally changes color by her mood; this week it's a gorgeous auburn brown. She has grey almond shaped eyes, deep dimples, and gorgeous caramel skin. All the girls agree that she is the most thoughtful, caring, and loving person, period! She has her ways, but no one loves harder than Asia, and that's a damn fact!

The girls constantly make fun of her mantra: I Don't Wanna Work (IDWW). Asia is no freeloader or gold digger, however. She has a great job as the Wellness Director for several day spas throughout the Los Angeles area, making great money, and is great at what she does. She simply doesn't want to work. She feels like working a 9 to 5 doesn't align with her chakras. Whatever that means. Lucky for her she has always dated successful men and hasn't had to work until recently.

Of course, she knew that she had to have a backup plan, so she graduated with a degree in Sociology and obtained her MBA, in the event her plan to not work anymore failed. Unfortunately for Asia, it has been the case, but not only is she well educated, she takes emotional and mental wellness seriously. She's the designated Zen Master when everything is chaotic. She helps the girls to get their chakras back in order. In addition to all that, Asia teaches private meditation and yoga classes for some of the wealthiest people in Los Angeles; she's the female Russell Simmons of the west coast and parts of the east coast, if you will.

"Ladies, this is the best night ever!" Asia says, full of enthusiasm.

Finally, we have the pretty, cold-hearted emotionless bitch of a workaholic! Yep, that's what people have called Kylisha directly to her face! Imagine what is said about her when she's not around. Standing tall at 5'10"with pretty milk chocolate skin, long hair that is currently ombre from black to dark brown to honey blonde, tied into a neat high bun tonight, she has big brown eyes with beautiful long natural lashes, perfectly arched eyebrows, a gorgeous smile, and flawless makeup. She, like Asia, is a gym rat, always working out at the gym or running laps at the park. Her long muscular legs and toned arms complement her very athletic physique.

Wearing a pair of blue, dark-washed distressed jeans, a mint green graphic tank that says "Diva's Do It Best" in hot pink showing off her shoulder and back tattoos, a clear Chanel cuff bracelet and strappy teal and gold Giuseppe's.

Most people call her Kyle, a trend that got started by her dad and sisters, and now has stuck. She started her first fashion magazine during junior year at college via the coaching of Evian, calling it FNBK (Fashion aNd Beauty by Kyle). Catchy, right? It started out as something for fun, to keep her creativity going, but has now reached to become the 5th most popular magazine in the world. Her favorite quote is, "My life is quiet chaos!", meaning life is chaotic but no one knows it but her. She always feels like she is putting out little fires at the magazine in secret. Whether it is stroking the ego of a featured designer who may or may not like how a shoot went, or sending hand written thank you cards to her featured celebs that grace the cover of her magazine.

Known for being too honest, if there's such a thing, aloof, and sometimes a little mean, as per her girls, Kyle is also the first one in line to support and endorse any endeavor you take on. While Tangi was still in school, Kyle got her a great job as head buyer for Neiman Marcus. She also had one of her writers interview Asia at her day spa to promote them, , which worked so well that business had to expand, all based off of the write up in FNBK.

When they were kids, Kyle, Asia, and Evian were like their own little clique. Even in high school, no matter what outside friends they may have had, if one of those outside friends stepped out of bounds with anyone in the clique, they could say goodbye to that friendship. They even followed each other to college, NYU, where they met Leslie. She and Kyle were line sisters for the same sorority.

It was Evian who introduced Tangi to the group. She was helping all the girls in Evian's dorm put outfits together on a budget, and the two immediately clicked. Not so long after, the five were inseparable. If you saw one, another wasn't far away. From college parties, sneaking into nightclubs, supporting Kyle and Leslie's step shows, or just in each other's dorms or apartments, they were always together. Of course, no group is perfect and the girls got into fights with and for each other every now and then, making them truly like sisters.

It was Kyle and Asia who set Leslie and Mike up in college. Mike lived in the same neighborhood, but went to a different school than the girls. He was like the big brother of the neighborhood, always sticking up for someone who he felt may be being bullied. The girls thought he would end up as a civil rights attorney. So when he chose corporate law, to say they were shocked is an understatement.

Kyle interrogated him for days, asking what made him make that choice, and in true lawyer fashion, he switched the conversation around to her. He asked her, "When your magazine becomes popular, won't you want an attorney you can trust to represent you and your brand,?" How could she argue with that? Asia made him promise that he would practice daily meditation to keep him grounded and keep his stress levels low.

She and Kyle would always brag about Leslie, telling him how they thought they would make a cute couple. When they finally met at a senior skate night, Leslie told Kyle she thought he was a jerk:

"Look at how he skates around with his pompous ass!" Leslie said.

Asia and Kyle looked at each other and laughed, "Girl, he is skating like everybody else", Asia said.

"No he isn't. He skates like he knows he is the man", Leslie said defensively in return, her arms folded and her face frowned up, "I am going to go out there and show his ass up." Leslie went out on the floor, skating and dancing backwards, rolling her eyes as she passed him.

The girls later found out that she and Mike had had several run-ins in their ethics class. Well, needless to say, that initial opinion changed about a month later, and the five ladies quickly turned into a group of four. Leslie was missing in action and the ladies were in full support of her absence. They loved Leslie and Mike together, so it was no surprise when it was announced they were going to attend the same law school. The way they saw it, two potential lawyers in the family is better than one.

"Congratulations, E!" they all screamed at Evian with their glasses up,

"Cheers to you girl, you're the baddest bitch I know!" screamed Asia, "and I don't just mean your looks, chica."

"Girl you have worked your ass off, and I can't think of a better closer than you", Leslie said.

"not to mention a better dressed closer", Tangi chimed in,

"Evian, I am so happy and proud of you! You are the shit!", Kyle yells with her glass up.

Evian, smiling from ear to ear, says, "I freaking love you guys, and there's no doubt without your encouragement, late night snacks, and jokes to keep me sane I would not have gotten this partnership", she says.

"Cheers!" they all scream in unison. "I am going to regret being out partying this hard this late, but how often do one of our closest girlfriends make partner at one of the largest sports management firms in the country?! No better reason to party in my book", Kylisha says as she takes another tequila shot.

The lights turn on in the club and all the ladies walk out into the night, Tangi and Asia stumble behind the rest of the ladies into the Lyft.

"Girl, when was the last time we shut a club down?", asks Tan.

"Girl, I don't know, maybe a year or two ago," Asia answers.

"I just want to thank you all for taking me out and celebrating with me, I really do love you guys", says E.

Crossing arms over the seats and each other in the SUV, they all have a group hug and automatically burst into drunken laughter.

Chapter 2

This is who I am....Kylisha Debrow

5:00am Buzz! Buzz! Buzz....

"There goes that damn alarm," Kyle thinks to herself as she turns over in bed to turn off her beeping phone.

"Just 20 more mins," is all she can think of. "I feel like hammered shit! Shots on a work night; that was just not a good idea at all. I just want to melt into my bed and stay asleep, but I know full well that I cannot even think straight if I don't go for my morning run."

"Ugh," she sighs, kicks the white goose down duvet off her and gets out of bed. "Wake up, girl! You gotta get this workout in!" she screams, walking to the bathroom.

She brushes her teeth, washes her face, and pulls her hair up into a messy bun. Looking at her sleepy self in the bathroom mirror, she debates on how to coordinate a workout outfit.

"I think I'll wear my purple and grey sport leggings, grey Nike sports bra, and my neon purple running shoes," she says.

Still feeling half in a daze she gets her workout clothes out of the dresser drawer, and sneakers out of the closet. Her phone rings, she laughs to herself when she sees who's calling.

"Hey Asia love," Kyle says.

"Hey girl, you going for your morning run?"

"As much as the thought of waking up this early to go run, especially being hungover annoys the shit out of me, yes, I am getting dressed to go."

"I know exactly how you feel. I'm on my way to the gym," Asia says.

"Once I'm out and start running I'll forget all about the extra 20 minutes of sleep that I was begging for," Kyle says.

"Exactly, so get out there, and I will call you later girl. Just wanted to check in on you. Love you."

"Love you too. Talk to you later hun."

Kyle hangs up, grabs her headset and plugs it into her phone, takes her keys off the hook by the front door, and heads out to her car.

She drives for about 15 minutes and parks and walks toward the trail to start her run.

"The cool air, the smell of the magnolia trees on the trail, and the sounds of my girl RiRi 'What's My Name?' blasting in my ears is all I need to get my morning started," Kyle thinks to herself as she starts her run. "Hmm…the trail's pretty empty this morning. Oh god! I spoke too soon! Here comes chatterbox Leo. I have to stop running this route.. Kyle, that's not nice, he helped you get home the day you fell and twisted your ankle–

"Hey Kyle!" says Leo, cutting off her thoughts.

"Hey Leo," Kyle says with the fakest smile ever, still jogging in place.

"I wish I would have known you were running this morning lady. We could have run together," Leo says.

"Oh yea, I like to get an early start before work. I like to clear my head before all the madness of the day begins."

"You mean the Grand Madame of the fashion magazine world can actually clear her thoughts?" he replies in a burst of laughter.

"As hard as it may be to believe, yes she can," Kyle says with a smirk and one eyebrow raised.

"Yeah, I totally get it. I like to get out early to start my day and then I'm set for at least half the day," Leo replies.

Standing tall at 6'5"with ashy blonde hair, slightly tanned skin, and in phenomenal shape –broad shoulders, muscular legs, and abs of steel – Leo is a very handsome guy

"I see you are not a fan of shirts," Kyle says.

"Nah, they get sweaty and sticky, so I just skip it," Leo says.

"You sure you aren't out here advertising for the ladies?" Kyle asks, then catches herself "OMG am I flirting with Leo?!" "Of course I am not, I do not even like him. He talks too much and seems like he'd be kinda needy."

"Me? No, not at all, I..."

"Relax, I'm just kidding with you Leo," Kyle says patting his arm.

"Omg, I'm doing it again! What the hell are you doing Kyle?! She thinks to herself."

Leo laughs, "I know, sometimes I take things too seriously. I'm Sorry."

"It's okay," Kyle responds. "Okay, end this conversation and get the hell out of here, Kyle! You're staring at him like he's dessert!" She thinks to herself.

"Okay, well I'll catch you later. I don't want to be late for work," Kyle says.

"Okay see you around," Leo says.

You've reached the end of your run, the running app on her watch informs. Kyle looks down at her watch. 6.0 miles in 50 minutes.

"Not too shabby," Kyle says to herself.

Kyle walks up the driveway and into her house after arriving back from the trail. She drinks a glass of water and hits the shower.

What shall I wear today? she thinks to herself while she is in the shower, going through her day in her head to determine what type of outfit will match.

I have several meetings with the team and then a viewing with a new designer. His line may be featured in our next issue. Let's see, maybe my black Kate spade sheath dress, grey Balmain blazer, my fuchsia, black and silver Hermès scarf, and my fuchsia suede Gucci pumps...Yes, that's it! Oh, and my new silver Chanel purse!

She poses in the mirror to showcase her outfit of the day, as if on some sort of invisible runway.

"Now this is a winner. Let's get it!" she says and smiles to herself.

She sits at the vanity in the bedroom and brushes her hair into a very neat high bun and applies her makeup.

"Today will have to be a less is more day," Kyle tells herself in the mirror as she finishes up.

Okay, am I going to drive in or call the car service...hmmm? Well I have errands to run after so I guess I will drive in. Plus, I can listen to that new Chris Brown album...God knows I love me some breezy!

As Kyle walks into the building once arriving at work she can hear the usual papers shuffling and phones ringing all around. Then hears someone whispering," She's here, your article on the Supreme Justices better be damn good or its going in the trash!" She walks by the receptionist and she answers the next call, "Good morning FNBK, how can I direct your call?"

"Good morning boss lady," says her assistant, Bethany. "I have your pomegranate black tea and fruit bowl at your desk. I am sure you have not stopped for breakfast, as usual. You must do better about eating in the morning, you know you can't function and by 11 you get all hangry on us in here. And uh, you look like you may need some Advil," she says with her face in a frown.

Kyle smiles," Thanks, Bethany. You know me too well. Wait, do I look that bad?"

"No, just a little tired," she says.

"I am beat, we celebrated Evian making partner a little too hard for a Thursday night," Kyle says.

"Oh wow! That's amazing news. Evian's finally made partner," Bethany says.

"Yes, I am so happy for her and proud of her. She has worked really hard," Kyle responds.

"Well, clearly you need to eat and get some caffeine and electrolytes into your system. I will grab you some Gatorade as well," says Bethany.

"What would I do if you weren't here?"

"Go crazy, starve and fire everyone that rubs you the wrong way." They both laugh.

"Yeah, that's true." Kyle says.

"Okay, so today you have a 10:00, 11:00, and a 12:30 meeting. Then you have the viewing with Shalon is at 2pm, 6 columns to read and approve, oh, and you have to decide what the theme for next month's issue and who will grace the cover."

Kyle rolls her eyes," Yes you're absolutely right, dammit! I guess I won't make it to run those errands after all." Looks like I will be here until the wee hours of the night with the way my day is looking so far. "Okay Bethany, get Shalon's look book ready for me and I'll need you in the meetings this morning and at the viewing at 2."

"Yes ma'am," Bethany says.

"Okay, let's get to it," Kyle says.

As Kyle prepares for her first meeting, she sips on her tea," Mmm, thank God for Bethany", she says to herself. She looks on her desk and sees the invite to the Tom Ford fall preview. I almost forgot all about that. Let me text Tan and see if she wants to go.

Kyle: Girl I got invited to attend the Tom Ford fall preview event, you in?

Tangi: Of course I'm in! Just let me know when and where and I will be there! Are all the girls coming?

Kyle: No. E is knee deep in work now that she's partner, Les will be out of town, and you know Asia, if it doesn't involve meeting an athlete, she ain't going...lol.

Tangi: LMAO, girl you know she's team IDWW, that girl is crazy...LOL!

Kyle: True that!

Tangi: Okay girl, thank you for the invite. I got to head off to meet with some clients and then I have a fitting.

Kyle: Okay girl, I will send you the event details later. Kisses <3

"I can't believe I got through three meetings and two long conference calls without passing out. This hangover is killing me, Kyle thinks to herself. Oh my god, today has been crazy. Can you do me a huge favor? I'll take you to dinner," Kyle says to Bethany with a huge smile, batting her long eye lashes in double time.

"What is it?" Bethany asks, raising one of her perfectly arched eyebrows up?

"Can you take my car home for me and grab me a change of clothes? Since I will be working late I can't stay in this all day. You can have the car service bring you back here for the 2 o'clock viewing with Shalon."

"Sure, no problem," Bethany says.

"Thank you Bethany. I swear you're the best assistant I could ever have asked for," Kyle says and gives her a huge hug.

Bethany heads directly to the garage to get Kyle's custom platinum silver Mercedes G wagon, loving every moment she gets the chance to drive it. She presses Start to turn on the engine and Chris Brown blasts through the speakers. With a surprised look on her face Bethany says, "What does Kylisha DeBrow know about Breezy?" laughing to herself. She pulls out of the garage bumping her head to the music. She drives for about twenty minutes and then arrives at Kyle's house, pulls out her cell phone and calls Kyle.

"Hey Bethany, what's up?" Kyle says when she answers

"I completely forgot to ask what you wanted to change into," says Bethany.

"Oh I am sorry, that's my fault, some sweats from the dresser, and my pink Ugg boots are fine.

"Okay got it, see you soon," says Bethany.

"Here you go boss lady," Bethany says after returning to the office just before 2, handing Kyle a bag of clothes and her keys.

"Thank you Bethany, you are amazing I owe you big! You ready for the 2 o'clock viewing?"

"Yes ma'am."

"Oh, by the way, Hermès sent me this bag, but it's not my color. Do you want it?"

Bethany looks at Kyle with the you know I do stare, "Uh, of course I do!" she replies

"Here you go. It's yours. Now let's get to this viewing. I have already tagged my favorite pieces, but overall, I am underwhelmed by his line. Unless he pulls out some surprises at this viewing, it's a no go for me."

"Well I guess you will find out in 5,4,3,2..." Bethany says. Laughing together, they head out to the company's private driver to go to the meeting.

They pull up to a huge studio in West Hollywood with enormous frosted glass windows with Shalon written across them. Shalon, a medium height, dark haired, white male, wearing a white t-shirt, shredded blue jeans, and black motorcycle boots, greets them at the door. Shalon explains that after some further walkthroughs with his models, he wasn't quite loving all the pieces and has changed things up quite a bit since the look book was sent out. Kyle looks a little annoyed, as she normally likes to see what changes are made prior to coming for a viewing. She and Bethany take a seat. As his models walk out one by one, Kyle takes notes, Hmmm...I am actually really pleased, she thinks to herself.

Once the viewing is over, Bethany tells Shalon that someone will be in contact to let him know what Kyle decides, that normally someone from the styling department will give him the details for the shoot, and one of the writers for the magazine will setup a time for the interview that will be featured in the issue, should he make the cut. Shalon thanks Kyle and Bethany for coming and considering him as he walks them out and to their car.

Driving back to the office Bethany confirms "You liked them, didn't you?"

"Yes I did, Kyle replies, "How'd you know?"

"I can read your face and know when it's a yes or a no."

Laughing, Kyle replies, "Yes, he will make a great feature for next month's issue. Give him a call first thing Monday morning and let him know it's a go. We'll send someone over to do the interview as well as a photographer to take some shots of some of his pieces, him in action and so on and so forth."

"Yes ma'am," says Bethany.

"Shalon is so down to earth and unpretentious, so likeable, which is hard to find in the fashion world, don't you think?" she asks Bethany.

"Yeah, he isn't like some of the designers we've worked with," says Bethany. "And it's not just the newbie thing, I think this is how he is on a normal basis."

"You can tell the ones that are on their way to cockyville," Kyle says. They both laugh. "His pieces were very edgy, but feminine, very sexy and flattering. I think people will love him and his designs," Kyle says. I agree, he had some nice stuff, Bethany replies.

"You know what? You can go ahead home, unless there is something you need from the office," Kyle says.

"Thanks! No, I have everything I need with me, Bethany says.

"Can you drop Bethany home before taking me back to the office please," Kyle asks the driver.

"Yes ma'am," the driver responds.

After about a ten-minute ride, "We're here," the driver announces.

"Okay ladybird, I will see you on Monday. I am headed back to the office to review those 6 articles, pick next month's theme, the cover layout and person of interest."

"Okay boss lady. Call me if you need anything," Bethany says.

"Will do. Have a great weekend."

Back at the office Kyle is knee deep in articles.

This will need to be re-written, but this one is good, she thinks. Okay, now on to the theme for the month. Hmmm, maybe some music will get my creative juices flowing.

She plays a Jill Scott song on her iPad.

"Come on, Jill, help your girl out," she says to herself as the music plays through the Bluetooth speakers.

"Let's take a long walk," Kyle sings and sways side to side, smiling to herself. "Okay, the cover story will be about Ladies of the Law, Fashionable Justice. We can use the new Supreme Justice as our cover/person of interest." She sits on the sofa, photos scattered all over, she carefully places them on her white board on the floor with sticky notes underneath each of them. "Okay, we are making some progress. I knew Jill wouldn't steer me wrong," Kyle says to herself. "The overall theme for the month…I still don't know. I guess I will be here all night until I figure it out. The quiet chaos begins. Holy crap! I didn't eat anything and it is going on 8:00pm. Bethany would nag the hell out of me if she knew I hadn't eaten yet," she says to herself. Let me call and have something delivered before I pass out because it is abundantly clear, I am not going home anytime soon."

Chapter 3

Girl Talk...

In attempt to save money while she began working on her own clothing line, and because she and Asia get along so well, Tangi asked Asia (who at the time was moving out of her NFL boyfriend Keith's house) if she wanted to be her roommate. Asia was here for it! She loves Tangi and it could give her time to save money and plot on her next move.

Tangi has an eye for style. She just knows how to put things together and makes her clients look amazing. Large or small budget doesn't matter, she will make you look like a million bucks even if it's just jeans, a t-shirt and a pair of sneakers. Kyle has told her multiple times that she have her own reality show called In My Closet.

As she sits in her office with piles of clothes strewn around it, she's in the middle of sketching talking to herself, along with going around putting outfits together and on racks and labeling them.

Tangi decided that she wanted to not only style her clients, she wanted to style them in her clothes. Her idea is to create entire outfits from hats to shoes that are already styled and sell them as an entire ensemble. She already created named categories for the project, her favorites including Werk It Girl, I'm the happiest this hour, Let's make it a date, and many others. Tan wants to make getting dressed easy for those that do not have the luxury or the resources of a personal stylist, but still have women feel stylish. She's not opposed to selling pieces separately, but those will be reserved for her current and future clients she styles in person. People in the fashion industry think she's a Godsend!

And now she has her very own live-in model, Asia, who just so happens to be her favorite model, mainly because she never tells her 'No'.

"Hey A, how was work today?" Tangi asks Asia as she walks in the apartment.

"Girl it was good. Trying to get the owner to invest in some better aromatherapy equipment for our treatment rooms. You would think with all the money that they pull in that would be a simple 'Yes', but no, not these cheap devils," says Asia. "I swear, I'm so over them! They are so worried about money."

"Umm everyone is, A," says Tangi. "Hell, we are roommates because I want to save money. The only person who isn't worried about money is you, silly goose," Tangi says as she taps her finger on Asia's forehead playfully. They both laugh.

"So Kyle invited me to a Tom Ford event. I'm thinking of asking her about featuring me and my line in next month's 'Who's Hot in Fashion' article," says Tangi.

"Isn't it a bit short notice?" asks Asia.

"She's the owner and Editor in Chief, she can get me in there," Tan responds.

"Girl, are you sure this is a good idea? You damn near came to blows when you quit that job she got you with Neimen's," Asia asks her with a confused look on her face. "Don't you remember? You were still in school at FIT when she got you the head buyer job and introduced you to some of your most loyal and still current clients, and within 60 days you quit!" Asia continues. "You said it wasn't your thing, whatever that means," she finishes, making air quotes shrugging her shoulders.

"Oh my god, don't remind me. I need you to be on my side A," Tan responds.

"I am on your side. I am on both of your sides. I just do not want to see you two fall out again," Asia explains.

"That was years ago. I think if I pick the right time and method of delivery it will be okay," Tan says.

"Kyle takes herself way too seriously sometimes, and gets all bent out of shape way too quickly. However, I do believe we are past that and in such a great place now that we can talk about it and not turn into a thing. As a matter of fact I am pretty sure she will say yes. I mean, I am one of her best friends and she's been dropping little jewels to people about my up and coming line," says Tan.

"Okay, let's hope so," says Asia with a hopeful look.

Ting! Ting! Ting!

"Oh Lord, who is this texting me? Tangi says to herself.

Leslie: Hey girl what are you doing? Feel like going to dinner? I need to get out this house for a minute. Mike is driving me bananas and I don't want this to turn into a fight.

Tangi: I was about to make something to eat. Wanna come over?

Les: If you are cooking, hell no!

Tangi: Angry emoji face, Girl I am so over you, you are the one that wants to get out the house.

Les: I will stay home and fight before I eat your cooking, Betty Crocker not. Laughing emoji.

Tangi: Fine, meet me at our spot in 5 mins.

Les: <3 Love you boo! Okay, see you there. Is A coming?

Tangi: I will ask.

Tangi: Yes she's coming, we will leave in 5 mins.

Les: Okay see you two in a bit.

"Thank God Les convinced you to come out for dinner. Girl you know you can't cook," Asia says.

"I can cook, you all just have bad taste buds," Tangi says, rolling her eyes at Asia.

"Well, you'd better ask Les or Kyle for some lessons, because clearly you're the one with the taste bud issue. Hell, even E can cook better than you. When a white girl can season her food better than you, Houston we have a problem," Asia laughs.

Les walks up to the table as Asia is cracking up laughing.

"What's so funny?" asks Les.

"Girl, Tan's cooking."

Les looks at Asia and Tangi and bursts out laughing, "You mean her ancient Chinese secret torture!"

Both Leslie and Asia are leaning over their seats in laughter, while Tangi just sits with her arms folded.

"You all are not funny," she says, unamused that she is the butt of the joke. "I hope you don't think I came out so you two heifers could laugh at me all night."

"Aww, okay don't be mad Tan, we are just playing. We love you girl," Les says. "But just know you have already cheered me up, I almost peed my pants laughing."

"Alright now, that's strike two," Tangi says.

"Okay, okay let's stop," says Asia. "What's going on in your world, Les?"

"We will need some wine for this story, let's get the waiter," Les says.

The waiter approaches the table.

"Can we have a bottle of the Caymus, please? Leslie asks.

"Caymus?! This is going to be a long dinner, says Asia.

"Well, you guys know I have been traveling like crazy for work these last few months. I am finally home for a good two weeks or so, and I am thinking I will make a nice dinner for Mike since he has been left to his own devices lately. So, I go grocery shopping, get his favorite food, his favorite wine, and I ran by Victoria's Secret," Les says with a mischievous grin.

"When I get home Mike is already home, which isn't normal. He usually works late. I ask him how his day was and what he thinks he may want for dinner, and he just starts going in on how he wants me to be home more, and accuses me of purposely turning down clients that would keep me home.

"Of course I am caught off guard because he has never, and I mean never complained or given me a hint that he had issues with my being gone so often. So I asked where this is coming from and how we can resolve this matter so that it doesn't become volatile. Well, that pissed him clean off. 'Don't handle me, I'm not one of your clients,' he says. So then I just got quiet, because he was yelling and I did not want to escalate things. I asked him calmly, 'Tell me what you need from your wife Mike?' He says nothing and storms into our bedroom. So now here I am with you all. I didn't know whether to stay and try and talk to him or leave, so I picked the latter."

'How long have the two of you been having fights like this?" Tangi asks.

"I don't know, the last couple of months have been rough for us. We are both working a lot and –

"Go home! Now!" yells Asia. "Wasn't your ass out with us last night shutting the club down, when you probably should've been with Mike? Girl, go home, make dinner, and then apologize for not hearing him, apologize for not knowing he needs you, and then just listen. Do not excuse or justify your absence, just listen. Go! Now! I will not sit at this table with you and have dinner when you should be home with your man, correction husband!" Asia says in a very stern tone.

"She's right," Tan says. "You gotta go home.

Now with tears in her eyes, Les says, "I am an idiot. I am such a bad wife."

"No you're not, you just forgot that sometimes he needs you too," says Asia. "Now take your crybaby ass to the restroom, wash your face, and go home. Tan and I will drink the wine and have a wonderful dinner."

"I love you two, you know that," Les says as she gets up from the table.

"We love you more mama," says Tangi,"Now git!" Asia and Tangi laugh as Leslie walks away.

"Okay girl, what are we eating?" Tangi asks looking at the menu.

"I don't know what I am eating, but I sure know I am drinking up this bottle of wine," Asia says with a grin on her face. They laugh together.

"Should we text Evian and see if she wants to join us? I know Kyle can't. We spoke earlier. She's working late on next month's issue," says Asia.

"Yeah, shoot her a text. I know she lives close by so it won't take her long to get here," Tangi responds.

Asia: Hey E, want to meet us at our spot for some dinner, wine, and conversation? I could use your help talking Tan off a ledge.

Evian: Sure! I'm just turning on my street. I'll just come there instead. Give me about 5 mins and I should be there. And what is Tan up to now? LOL.

Asia: She is thinking of asking Kyle to feature her in next month's 'Who's Hot in Fashion' article, distressed emoji.

Evian: Wait what? Surprised emoji. I can't, I'm gonna crash. I cannot focus, I will see you when I get there.

"She is on her way," Asia says.

"Okay cool. So let's just get a water for her and some appetizers until she gets here," Tangi says.

"Hey ladies, Evian says, arriving a few minutes later. She walks to the table giving hugs to both women. "Happy Friday! I cannot believe I am even awake, no less able to come out and eat and drink after last night."

"Oh my god!" Asia sighs, "I drank nothing but spa water all day today, and then had to lead a meditation class due to one of the instructors deciding to call out last minute."

"You two should be ashamed of yourselves, carrying on like two elderly ladies complaining about being out for the first time in probably months. Last night was the bomb! And I for one miss those days," Tangi says, shaking her head with her arms folded across her chest.

"So how goes life for the most called upon Stylist in the country? asks Evian. "I heard you were styling for several shows this year at New York's fashion week."

"You heard that right. And with the help of my magazine mogul, maybe I can get a spot of my own for my line," says Tangi.

"Oh wow! Kyle is helping you secure a fashion week spot?" Evian asks, winking at Asia.

"Well, not directly. I was planning on asking her to feature my line in next month's issue of 'What's Hot in Fashion'," Tangi says with a huge smile on her face.

"Wait, I thought the two of you agreed for the sake of your friendship that you two would never ask or give business favors again, due to the whole Neiman's debacle," Evian queries.

"Neiman's, Neiman's, Neiman's! I swear you all won't let me live without bringing that bullshit up," Tangi yells.

"Okay first, let's use our inside voice, Second, I am only stating the facts, Tan. Kyle and you didn't speak for a year over it," Evian explains. "Do you really want to risk your friendship with her? You two have been through a lot together and I would hate for that to go left over a favor," Evian says while grabbing Tangi's hand.

"You guys, Kyle and I are good, we have both matured. Not to mention, you all know her magazine is like the Oprah of the fashion world. One endorsement from her magazine and BOOM, you're in. How do you think I got all the high-profile clients I have? Kyle! Plus, she was the one who extended the offer of a write up in her magazine," Tan responds.

"Wait so she already offered 'Who's Hot in Fashion' to you? Asia asks.

"No, she offered me a spot in the 'Cutting Edge of Style' section.

"Okay, I am utterly confused," Evian says.

"I don't want to be in the 'Cutting Edge of Style', I don't think that will generate enough attention to my line," Tan explains.

Asia rolls her eyes, "So instead, you're going to ask for one of the cover stories, and last minute? Asia asks

"Yes. Listen ladies, I truly believe we are past the big Neiman's scandal that everyone loves to revisit," Tangi says sarcastically. "She has been so great about telling folks about my upcoming line, I know it will be fine."

"Okay, I'll let it go and only speak positive energy into the situation," Asia says.

"Get that spot at Fashion Week girl! And go be great, as Kyle would say," says Evian, holding her wine glass in the air. The ladies share the toast and say, "I'll drink to that," in unison.

Chapter 4

In Love and War...

Leslie pulls into the garage after arriving home after the restaurant. Looking in the rearview mirror, she tells herself," Go in there and go apologize." She walks into the house and goes to the bedroom. No Mike. The kitchen, no Mike. The living room, no Mike. She goes back in the kitchen and sees a note on the fridge:

You left, so I went to have a couple of drinks with the guys. I don't want to fight, I was wrong and I am sorry. I will be back.

Leslie falls to the floor and cries, "No, I was wrong and stupid," she says to herself.

****

Half sleep now in her usual sweats and pink Ugg boots, with her hair in a ponytail, Kyle is sitting on the loveseat in her office, still going over articles and photographs spread across the coffee table. As she makes notes on her white board, her phone rings. "Hey Mike, what's up? Where's Les and where's my plate? I heard she was going to be cooking up a storm, asks Kyle.

"Hey Kyle, tell me you're not still at work. I need to talk to you. It's important. Can I swing by?"

"Of course. I am still at work. Is everything okay? Is Les okay? Kyle asks.

"Yes, Les is okay. I need your advice. We had a little blow up and I just need a friend. You're the only one who knows us both and who I know will tell me the truth," Mike says.

"Okay, come on through. Have the security guard call me so you can get in or else he will escort you right on out the door being it's well pass 10pm. I am knee deep in work but I can take a break for a friend," Kyle says.

"Thanks Kyle. I will see you shortly," says Mike. About 15 minutes pass before the security guard buzzes Kyle.

 "Ms. DeBrow, are you still in? You have a visitor," a voice says over the intercom.

"Yes, I'm here. Let him up, thank you, Kyle replies.

"Knock, knock," Mike says, appearing at the door.

"Boy, come on in here. The door is open! Were you already in the garage? I literally just hung up the damn phone, Kyle says.

"Yeah, I was. I had a feeling you were still working. You've never known when to go home and call it quits for the day. Even when we were little you were always way too engulfed in things to the point you forgot, 'Hey, this is supposed to be fun'. When freeze tag turns into work, Houston we have a problem," Mike says laughing.

"Shut up. I was not that damn bad," Kyle says.

"Kyle, I think I am losing my mind. I went ham sandwich on Leslie. I didn't mean to, I just got so upset."

"Okay, so tell me what happened. And don't lie to me Mike," Kyle warns.

"I won't, shit I can't. You will see right through it if I do," Mike says. "So, Leslie came home, and asked me how my day went and what I wanted for dinner. We were talking, everything was normal, until she said she was planning a trip to London to meet with a new potential client. I just went left. I accused her of taking on clients that she knew would prevent her from being able to be home, told her she was selfish, and needed to do some research on what a marriage consist of, because leaving your husband to fend for himself isn't it," he explains. "She stayed calm and attempted to talk it out, but I told her don't try and handle me like I am one of her clients. She asked me what I needed from her, I said nothing and stormed the fuck off. "I know I was wrong, but I hate when she gets all quiet and then tries to handle me," Mike says.

"Okay, is it my turn?" Kyle asks.

"Kyle, just talk man," Mike says with his face in his hands.

"First thing's first, pick up your face. Second, watch your tone brotha, I will still stomp a mud hole in your chest, I promise. I got sneakers and a jar of Vaseline in my work closet just for the occasion."

Mike smiles, "Girl you still think you can beat everybody."

"Now let's start with how you said what you said. I am sure that it wasn't the content of what you said that caused this whole thing to escalate. Mike, you don't know how to talk to people when you get in your feelings. You get all loud and do not articulate things in a way that make people listen. They either go on the defense or clam up. You know your wife, she is not the confrontational type outside of the workspace, so why would you even approach any discussion with all that bravado? Yes, she travels quite a bit, but so do you," Kyle says.

"Kyle, that is where you are wrong. I have decreased the amount of traveling I do immensely," Mike explains.

"What is the real problem Mike? Is everything okay at work?" asks Kyle.

Work is fine, busy as hell, but good. I'm ready to be a dad Kyle, and I don't think Leslie wants to start a family," Mike confesses. I honestly think she is content with our current situation and has zero desire to change it.

"Have you two talked about having kids?" Kyle asks.

"Kind of, but whenever we get on the topic, she starts talking about how demanding work is right now and how she has so much on her plate. I end up feeling bad and just change the subject. Do you think Leslie is happy in our marriage Kyle?

"Absolutely! Of course she is! Leslie loves you so much," Kyle says.

"Do you think maybe she has met someone else?" Mike asks.

"No, she would never do that. Les is a good girl, one of the most loyal people I know," Kyle responds reassuringly. "She'd die before she'd intentionally hurt someone she loves."

"You're right, I'm tripping. I just love her so much, and I want her to be happy, but I can't deny the fact that I am ready to be a dad. I am so ready to see her with the pregnant woman glow," Mike says. "I'm just ready for us to enjoy life and each other in opposed to working our asses off all the time, especially since now we do not have to anymore. This whole thing has me feeling like I am a crazy person.

"You're not crazy," Kyle says. "I understand how you feel, and I think you guys need a weekend away from here alone to talk, and I mean really talk," Kyle says.

"That is a good idea. Well, I'll let you get back to work. I know how busy you are. Thanks for listening and thanks for telling me the truth. I am going to go home," Mike says.

"Anytime. I am never too busy for my friends, you know that. Now go home and apologize to your wife, #my friend," Kyle says.

"Kyle, no one wants to hear your hashtags this late at night. I'm out. Later," says Mike as he leaves.

"I better call Leslie and see if she's okay," Kyle says to herself as she dials the number. "Dammit! She's not answering! I'll text her and let her know Mike was here."

Kyle: Hey Les, Mike just left here. I wanted to check in on you and make sure you were okay. Call me in the morning. Luv you!

"Guess I'll take my ass home now. God knows no more work is getting done now," Kyle says to herself, and then remembers, "Dammit! The car service isn't going to come this late! Shit! What now? Let me text E and see if she's still up. Maybe she can come get me."

Kyle: Hey E you up?

Evian: Hey girl, yes on my way home. Just leaving dinner with A and Tan.

Kyle: Girl, I'm here at work and forgot the car service closes down after 11.

Evian: On my way! Happy face emoji

Kyle: <3

Evian pulls up 10 minutes later in front of FNBK.

"Oh my god, thank you so much for picking me up E, I owe you," I did not feel like dealing with a chatty Lyft or Uber driver, says Kyle as she hops into the passenger seat.

"Girl, no you don't. You are always giving me clothes and shoes, getting me into elite parties, art gallery openings, and stuff. I probably owe you like a million rides home," Evian says laughing.

"I am beat. Today was crazy! How was your day ? Kyle asks.

"It wasn't too bad, actually. Got off early and had dinner with Asia and Tan."

"Are you off tomorrow? Feel like staying over and watching movies and homemade brunch and mimosa's in the morning? Kyle asks as Evian pulls up to her house.

"Now you know I cannot turn down your cooking or mimosa's! I'm in!

"Awesome, I'll get you something to sleep in and set the guest room up for you," Kyle says. "What do you want to watch?"

"Hmm, that's a good question. Let me think...I don't know. Let's just scan through the channels and pick something," Evian responds.

"So Mike came by the office, maybe 20 minutes before I texted you," says Kyle's she hands Evian a pair of pj's.

"Why? And why so late?" asks Evian.

"Well, originally I didn't think anything of it. I was just like, 'What's up? Where's Les and my food?' since I know Les was cooking. Then he was like, could he come through it was important, then I was like what's up because it's late and secondly what's wrong? I thought something was wrong with Les. He was like, he needed my advice, so I said sure come on through. Well, long story short, they had an argument, solely started by Mike, and I let him know it was his fault. Basically, he wants to have kids, and he thinks Les doesn't, due to the fact that she's taking on more work to avoid being home," says Kyle.

"Wow, do you think it's true? Leslie has been taking on a boat load of work lately and has been M.I.A a lot," asks Evian.

"I don't know. I asked Mike if he and Les have had the baby conversation, and he said kind of. I have never heard Les say she doesn't want kids. She is super driven and focused on making their firm self-sufficient. I do not think she is purposely staying away from home," Kyle concludes.

"Well, I hope everything works out okay for them. I love them together," Evian says.

"They'll be fine. They just need to have a real heart to heart talk about what their needs are, and how they can both get what they need from each other," says Kyle.

"You're right. Now let's get to this movie lady," Evian says.

"Okay, I'll get some snacks. You know we can't watch TV without snacks."

****

1:00am Mike walks into the house. Leslie is asleep on the couch with the television on.

"Leslie," Mike whispers.

Leslie doesn't move. Mike turns the TV off, puts a blanket over her, and lays on the other side of the couch and goes to sleep.

8:00am Mike kisses Leslie on the forehead

"Good morning sleepy head. I made you some coffee.

Leslie smiles as she replies,"Good morning my love. What do you want for breakfast? she asks as she gets up and walks towards the kitchen.

"I will let you surprise me," Mike says. "Leslie, I want to apologize for my behavior yesterday. I shouldn't have spoken to you in that way. I have a lot I want to say to you, and I think I just let my frustration get the best of me," he says, holding Leslie's hand in his.

"No, it's me that owes you an apology. I will make us breakfast and let's talk. I mean, really talk about what's on your mind," Leslie says.

"Okay, I'm going to jump in the shower, and then we can talk, cool? asks Mike.

Leslie nods her head yes.

Leslie walks over to grab her phone and starts scrolling through her texts. "Oh, Kyle texted me. I thought Mike was out with his friends?" Leslie whispers to herself.

Leslie: GM Kyle, I'm okay, thanks for checking on me. I will give you a call a little later.

Kyle: GM beautiful! Okay. I am just over here about to make me and E brunch, so I am here, call me whenever.

Leslie: Okay I will, you and E enjoy brunch If you are cooking I know it will be good. Kisses

Kyle: Kisses to you

Leslie turns some music on and starts cooking breakfast. "Let's see, maybe some eggs, bacon, chocolate chip croissants, fresh fruit, and that brunch punch Kyle taught me to make," Leslie says to herself.

"It is smelling good in here babe," Mike says as he dances his way to the kitchen.

"I see that two step is still working for you," Leslie says laughing. Boy don't make me come out this kitchen and show you something," she says, snapping her fingers and swaying side to side.

"Come out here and show me what you got," Mike says.

"I don't think you're ready for this," Leslie teases, coming out the kitchen dancing with a spatula in her hand.

The duo laugh as they dance together in the living room.

"Okay, let me get back to cooking before the fire alarm goes off, plus I don't want to show you up in here," Leslie says winking at Mike.

"Yeah okay, you wish you could show me up," Mike says.

"Listen dance fever, can you set the table since you have so much energy?" Leslie asks.

"Yes ma'am," Mike laughs and starts setting the table.

Leslie brings the food over to the table along with a pitcher of punch.

"Oh hell!" Mike says surprised, "Not that dangerous brunch punch.

Leslie laughs, "Well, you better sip it slow lightweight. See, this is what I miss." I can't remember the last time we just had fun and laughed like this. Things have been so tense, and have felt so forced lately. How did we get here?

"I'm not sure, but I do know us not talking about the tension and acting like it will go away on its own has not helped," Mike replies. "Let me start by apologizing again babe. Yes, I was frustrated, and had things on my chest that needed to be said. However, my method of delivery was off. I should have never raised my voice at you. Please forgive me," Mike says taking Leslie's hand into his. "I just feel like sometimes we are on two different paths in our marriage. I am ready for us to start a family, slow down, enjoy the fruits of all of our hard work. And it seems like that's the furthest thing from your mind right now," Mike expresses.

"We both agreed when we started our firm five years ago, that once it became somewhat self-sufficient, we would pull back from the litigating and negotiation roles, and only take on high priority or special request clients. I have done my part in scaling back, but you seem to be taking on more clients, and none of late have been local."

"I know. You're right, things have been very tense lately, and I have been taking on more clients, but you know as well as I do that we are so close to signing the Alina Media firm as a full time client, and the only way to get them hook, line, and sinker is to travel to their offices. Signing them would put us in a space where I wouldn't have to go out of town anymore unless there were some sort of unforeseen emergency. They would be our first, but hopefully not our last international client. I didn't realize that you feel how you do. I thought you got what I was trying to do. When you first were pursuing FNBK as a client, you constantly had to work late and travel with Kyle to gain her trust and her business. This is exactly the same scenario," Leslie explains.

"When we were pursuing FNBK we were still small. We only had three large big-name clients at the time. We are now one of the largest firms on the west coast, so it's a bit different," Mike replied. "Furthermore, you said the same thing last year when you were signing that private jet company. You said after them, you would slow down and scale back, and that their business would make it possible. Well, we have had them as a client for a year, and you are still full throttle, what am I supposed to think when this is a pattern with you?" Mike asks. "You say you will slow down, and then find a new big fish to hook. Do you think my local clients do not request for me to travel more frequently? Of course they do. Kyle is always asking me can I fly out somewhere with her, and I don't, I send another associate. Or I will have her conference me in on the meeting," Mike explains. "In order for me to agree to travel, there has to be a huge necessity for my physical presence."

"What's with the name dropping Mike?" Leslie asks.

"Huh?" Mike says with a confused look on his face.

"We have several clients, demanding ones too. But you keep pulling Kyle's name out of your ass! And what were you doing over her house so late last night? Your note said you were going out with the boys. Since when is Kyle the "boys"?" Leslie demands.

"Wait, are you serious right now? You are the one who brought her up," Mike says. "What exactly do you think is going on between Kyle and I Leslie?" Mike inquires.

"I have no fucking idea Mike. That's why I'm asking you!" Leslie yells.

"I am not going to argue with you about Kyle Leslie. As a matter of fact, I'm not going to sit here and go back and forth with you at all," Mike says getting up from the table. "I wanted us to have a rational discussion about our marriage, and you are going somewhere crazy," Mike responds. "If you weren't ready to talk, you should have said so, but to attempt to throw accusations around, nope I am not engaging in this. And just so you know, I was with my boys last night, but I also stopped by to talk with Kyle at her office, not her house," Mike clarifies. "It's mighty clever of you to flip the script when we are talking about you. I'm out!"

Mike walks away from the table, grabs his keys off the wall hook, and leaves out the front door.

"You did it again! What the hell is your problem?! Stop him. Go outside and get him," Leslie says to herself, but never moves from the table.

Chapter 5

Chicken, Waffles & Karaoke....

"Good morning E. I'm going to text Asia and Tan to see if they want to come over for brunch," Kyle says.

"You know Asia is coming," Evian says laughing.

(Group text)

Kyle: Asia and Tan, wake up! Brunch at my house....you in or out? E is already here.

Asia: Leaving in 5,4,3,2...LOL and I'm coming in my jammies.

Tangi: Look at greedy! So you're not going to shower? You're just gonna run out all smelly in your PJ's... LOL!

Kyle: LMAO!!!!

Asia: Bitch, I don't smell, A! And B, Kyle has a shower and I will bring a change of clothes, so go get your life!!!

Tangi: I'm going to shower and I'll be over. Asia, you can go without me, since you can't wait to eat.

Kyle: Well, you two figure it out and I will see you both when you get here. Smooches! And can one of you please bring me some lemons.

Asia: I got you.

Kyle: Thanks.

"Tan, you want to ride together or do you have something to do after brunch?" Asia asks.

"Yeah, you can go ahead without me. I have to go look at a new space for my studio later today," Tangi replies.

"Okay, I will see you there. Don't take all day, you know you are always running late," Asia says.

"Shut up, smelly! I will be right behind you," Tangi says, peeking her head out of the bathroom door.

"Whatever heifer," Asia says as she flips Tangi the middle finger and walks out the door.

Asia pulls up to Kyle's house and walks inside.

"Girl, you are looking for someone to come in here and rob, attack, or murder you. Why don't you lock your damn door?" Asia asks walking towards the kitchen with lemons in one hand and a huge tote bag in the other.

Kyle and Evian laugh.

"Girl, you were not lying when you said you were coming in your jammies and a bag," Evian says.

"The second guest room and bathroom are all set up for you A. All your special spa stuff is in there too," Kyle says laughing as she cuts up potatoes in the kitchen.

"See, that's why I love you Kyle. So thoughtful and accommodating. About thirty minutes later Asia walks out of the guest room. It smells good here, what are you cooking?" Asia asks, grabbing a glass of champagne off the counter.

"There's orange, cranberry, and pineapple juice in the fridge for you to make your mimosa. I am making French toast casserole, breakfast potatoes, eggs, bacon, and sausage," Kyle replies.

"Yes!!! I can't wait," Asia says. "When did you get here E?

"Oh, I've been here since last night. I picked Kyle up from work and stayed over," Evian replies.

"Wait, where was my sleepover invite, chica? Asia asks

"Girl, it wasn't planned. Get over yourself," Kyle responds laughing.

"Where's Tan? Running late as usual," Kyle asks.

"Yep, you know she is late for everything," Asia says.

"I hear you bitches talking about me," Tangi says as she walks in the kitchen smiling.

"Hey girl, it's about time! You only live ten minutes away," Evian says.

"Please! The food isn't even ready yet, and unlike you ladies, I like to put myself together before leaving the house," Tangi replies doing a twirl in her beautiful white sundress, royal blue fedora, and yellow sandals. It smells so good in here Kyle. I see you doing your thing."

"Thank you. You look stunning by the way. You walked in right on time for a change. The food is almost done, Kyle says. Her phone suddenly goes off.

"Girl, your phone's always going off," Asia remarks.

"Yeah, and it's usually one of you heifers," Kyle responds picking up her phone from the counter. She sees it's a text from Mike.

Mike: Kyle what did you say to Leslie? She has lost her damn mind!

Kyle: Huh? I haven't spoken to Les today. She texted me earlier saying she was okay and would call me later.

Kyle: I texted her last night, to let her know you had just left so she wouldn't worry. That's about it. Why? What's going on?

Mike: She's tripping. I tried to talk to her and she just flipped the script.

Kyle: What the hell happened?

Mike: I'm going to a hotel. I'll call you later.

Kyle: Okay, are you sure you're okay?

Mike: No, but I need to clear my head and think.

Kyle: Okay. I understand. Go cool off.

Mike: I will call you later, but just know I listened and it still went left.

Kyle: Go cool off and we will talk later.

Just as she's about to put the phone back down it begins to ring.

"Hey Les."

"Hey, can I come by? I did something stupid and don't feel like being home alone," Leslie says.

"Of course. All the girls are here," Kyle says.

"Good, I need to be around my girls today. I'll be over in about an hour," Leslie says.

"Okay hun. I'll see you then," Kyle says and hangs up. "Les is on her way guys," she announces.

"Yay!" the girls yell together.

"Is it time to eat yet? Asia asks.

"Yes, but let me set everything up in the back by the pool. We can eat out there and get some sun and chat, says Kyle. "Tan, can you program the outdoor speakers for me and hook them up to my iPad via Bluetooth so we can listen to some music out here? You know I don't have a clue how to set it up.

"Girl, of course! You spent all that money to have them make you pool area into an outdoor living room and can't set up any of your electronics? Damn shame, Tangi responds laughing, and goes over to set up the sound. Done! See how easy and fast that was Tan says as music starts to blast out into the pool area.

Kyle flips the middle finger at her in response.

"Okay, ladies. Help yourselves!" Kyle announces.

"Thank God! I was starving," says Asia.

"You are always hungry and always eating. Be careful y'all, you know she'll knock you down to get to the food first!" Tangi yells.

"You damn right, I sure will! So everybody best move out my way," Asia admits. "Wait, where's the chicken and waffles? Asia asks, staring at the array of food on the table.

"Who said anything about chicken and waffles." Kyle asks.

"There's no brunch without your famous chicken and waffles Kyle!" Asia responds.

"Well, I wasn't aware that there was a standard set for brunch food, A" Kyle says laughing.

"Yeah Kyle. I was ready for some chicken and waffles too!" Tangi yells while she picks up the remote for the sound system and turns the music up.

"Well, too bad so sad! No chicken and waffles today ladies," Kyle responds. "I can always throw all this out and–

"Hold on! You're going too far," Asia interrupts. "I never said I didn't want what we have, I was just looking for the chicken and waffles. Let's not get ahead of ourselves now," she says while finishing up putting food on her plate, she takes a seat at the table. All the ladies laugh.

"Oh wow! I don't think I have ever sat out here," Asia says. It's beautiful. Waterfalls, outdoor TV, and sofas. Just stunning.

"Well, Ms. Workaholic had it built so she could work from home and be comfortable, but you gotta leave work and go home to work from home," Tangi interjects.

Kyle rolls her eyes.

"This is so good! I have to get you to teach me to cook," Evian says.

"No, she needs to give Tan some cooking lessons. God knows she needs them," Asia jokes.

"Alright, you're not going to keep talking about my cooking," Tangi says.

"Or lack thereof. Tan, you can't even use the microwave," Kyle chimes in laughing.

Tangi rolls her eyes and flips the middle finger to the girls.

"Hey girls, where are you at?" Leslie yells as she walks in the door.

"We're in the back," Kyle yells. Leslie walks toward the pool area, "Hey!" she yells.

"Hey lady!" Evian gets up and gives her a hug. "You hungry?"

"No I actually just ate at home," Leslie responds.

"Thirsty? Asia asks, holding up a glass.

"Yes, definitely need a drink," says Leslie.

"I'm going to change. Clearly I was thirsty, pointing to a wet spot on her shirt. I spilled my drink all over my damn shirt," Kyle says.

"Can I get a pair of socks? You know you keep this house too damn cold," asks Leslie.

"Yeah, come pick a pair out," Kyle responds, knowing Leslie really just wanted a minute alone with her.

"Kyle, I owe you an apology," Les says as they walk into Kyles's bedroom.

"An apology? Why? Kyle asks.

"I will make this short and sweet cause I don't want the girls running in here. I threw your name into the middle of Mike and I's argument this morning. I didn't mean to, it just kind of came out," Leslie professes.

"I'm not going to ask what was said, I'm just going to say, if it had anything to do with him being at the office last night, he only came to talk about you, and ask for my honest opinion. I told him he was dead wrong for how he communicated with you, and told him he owed you an apology."

Tears start to come down Leslie's face.

"Les, you have nothing to cry about, I am not mad, I promise," says Kyle, wiping the tears from Leslie's face.

"Girl, I am an emotional mess, and I think I know why," Leslie says.

"Now, I know you don't want to talk about it, so wipe your eyes, put on some socks and let's see if some bubbles and girl chat will cheer you up," Kyle says as she hugs Leslie and kisses her on the cheek. Leslie pulls a pregnancy test out of her back pocket, and gives it to Kyle.

"Oh my god you're pregnant!" Kyle whispers.

"I literally just found out," Leslie says wiping her face. "I have been feeling crazy lately, and Mike and I have been having some pretty wild nights," Leslie says.

"Are you excited?" Kyle asks

"I am scared to death! Please don't mention this to Mike or the girls. I need a moment to get over the shock of it," Leslie says.

"I wouldn't dream of opening my mouth about this. It's not my place," Kyle says. "Well, fix your face and let's get back to the ladies before they start getting nosey.

"Okay, thank you Kyle," Leslie says. Kyle winks at her and starts laughing.

"We were just talking about Tan's cooking," Kyle says as they walk back outside .

"Or lack thereof," Leslie says giggling. All the girls bust out into laughter.

"I am so glad I have things to do, because I will not be the topic of discussion today," Tangi says as she gathers her purse to go to the gate that leads to the front driveway.

"Wait, you're leaving already? Asia asks.

"Yeah, unfortunately I have to go look at that new space, but I will call later. If you all are still here I'll come back. Maybe I'll even cook for you," Tangi jokes as she closes the gate behind her.

"Bye Tan!" the girls yell.

"So how's work been going Kyle? Leslie asks.

"So busy. It's spring, and trying to come up with innovative ways to be different then every other fashion publication is exhausting, but I love my work.

"And your love life? Evian asks.

"My what? Oh yeah, that doesn't exist," Kyle says rolling her eyes.

"Kyle, you have to get over Patrick and start dating again. It's been almost 2 years since you two broke up," Leslie says.

"I know, I am trying guys, I swear I am. The thought of dating makes me so tired," Kyle says. I'm just not sure I have the energy to throw myself into the dating pool. Speaking of pool, I'm going to change into a swimsuit and get in the pool if anyone wants to join me. We can resume the conversation when I return."

"I'll just sit on the edge and wet my feet," Leslie says.

"I'll grab a suit out of my old room, I am sure there is one still in there." Evian says.

"Asia, you want me to bring out some choices for you? You can change in the pool house if you want, Kyle says.

"You read my mind. Thank you girl," Asia replies.

"Leslie, how about you?" Kyle asks. "You know my closet is pretty much a fitting room/sample closet.

"Sure, thanks Kyle," Leslie responds. Kyle walks back into the house.

"Okay, I'm back," Kyle says as she hands several bathing suits to Asia and Leslie. She eases into the water and hangs on the side of the pool facing the girls.

"Seriously Kyle, have you given up on dating?" Evian asks

"No, not at all. I am just not sure how to even go about meeting a man anymore."

"Have you thought of maybe trying a matchmaker?" Evian asks.

Kyle rolls her eyes and sinks to the bottom of the pool. Both Leslie and Evian shake their heads and laugh. When she comes up for air,

Kyle gasps, "I know it worked for you in the past, but what if you are the exception to the rule? What if I end up with some weirdo mama's boy with no job, #disaster? Kyle asks.

"Oh, Lord! She's starting with the hashtags," Leslie says.

"No, seriously guys. What if he's a total jerk off? Kyle asks.

"Well, then you don't date him," Leslie says shrugging her shoulders.

"Maybe you just need some random hook ups to start," Asia says from under a huge sun hat as she sits up on the lounge chair. "Maybe if you have that car serviced you won't be so antsy about dating cause sex will not be an issue. There is nothing wrong with having a good old-fashioned maintenance man."

"She has a point. Maybe dusting off the cobwebs may help you," Evian says as she dives into the water."

"Well, well, well! Look who has awaken from their brunch nap," Leslie says looking at Asia.

"I wasn't napping, I was relaxing and listening to you all," Asia says sticking her tongue out at Leslie.

There's a knock on the gate.

"Are you expecting anyone? Asia asks.

"No," Kyle responds.

"How did anyone know we were back here?" Evian asks

"Maybe the music or the note I put on the door in case Tan comes back," Asia replies.

"Note?" Kyle asks.

"Yeah, it said "Tan, we are in the back. Just come thru the side gate", Asia responds.

"Well, let me go see who it is," Kyle says. She walks to the gate with water dripping everywhere.

"Leo!" Kyle says in utter surprise.

"Hey Kyle, I wanted to stop by and drop off an invitation to the art gallery opening next Friday," Leo says. I was going to just drop it in your mailbox, but I saw the cars parked out front and heard the music, so I figured I would give it to you in person."

"Is this for that new artist everyone has been raving about?" Kyle asks.

"Yeah, it is," Leo responds.

"Wow, thanks! I was trying to get tickets to that. I waited too long and they were sold out, and I haven't had the time to reach out to any of my contacts. I would love to go," Kyle says.

"Well, I know that on one of our quick park discussions you mentioned you liked art and attend as many showings as time allows, so when I was invited to attend as a special guest, I figured you'd be the best person to ask to go with me," Leo responds.

Not knowing what to say or how to honestly feel about all the flattery Leo was giving her, Kyle quickly changes the direction of the conversation before she starts flirting unconsciously with him again.

"Oh my god, I am being so rude. Leo, these are my girlfriends, this is Leslie, Evian, and Asia," Kyle says.

"Hello ladies, I am so sorry to intrude on your day," Leo says as he waves his hand and smiles at them.

"Hey Leo," the girls say in unison.

"Well, I will let you get back to your relaxing day and I'll see you on the trail Monday morning," Leo says.

"Okay, thanks again. Have a good weekend," Kyle says as she smiles at Leo and closes the gate.

"Ummm, okay who was that hot piece of man meat?" Asia asks.

"Who, Leo?" Kyle asks with her face scrunched up. "We see each other all the time on the trail when I go for my runs."

"Yeah, but how does he know where you live?" Asia asks, standing with an eyebrow raised, hands on her hips and tapping her toe on the pavement.

"Oh, remember that day I fell and hurt my ankle running?" Well Leo was the person who drove me home," Kyle replies.

"And he stopped by for?" Leslie asks

"Oh, to invite me to that new artist's show that we all were talking about last week at dinner," Kyle replies nonchalantly.

"Wait, Leo? The world renowned chef? The same Leo that everyone has been talking about and that every woman dreams about? Evian asks. "The same Leo who carried you to your car, then drove you home in your car, and then caught a Lyft back to his?"

All eyes are on Kyle now.

"Yes, that is the same person," Kyle says rolling her eyes. "Why are you guys looking at me like that?

"Girl, if you don't know, we sure aren't going to explain it to you. Somebody set up the karaoke machine, I've had enough of this Tom Foolery," Asia says, and walks into the house.

Chapter 6

The Situationship....Kyle and Patrick

Kyle and Patrick met about six months after moving FNBK's team headquarters to Los Angeles. At this point her magazine had created a huge buzz, selling off the shelves and online like crazy. Once construction was complete on the new headquarters, Kyle reached out to a friend of hers to find a good IT company to set up her infrastructure. She needed computers, telephones, computer hardware, software, semiconductors, internet, telecom equipment, e-commerce and a plethora of other tech services.

At the same time, she was running around trying to find a good interior designer to make her vision for her new home and office come to life. On one of several busy days at the new office, Kyle was walking a potential interior designer, Monique through the building, explaining what she wanted.

"So I have the top six floors of the building. We are on the 30th through the 35th floor," Kyle said. "Our beauty department will be on the 30th floor. As you can see, we will have several stations where our beauty team can stock their kits, but we will also have a studio in the back for product shoots," she continued. "I want this area to be ultra-glam, with mirrored furnishings, gorgeous sparkling chandeliers, white leather chairs and sofas, maybe even a mirrored floor in some areas."

"And the colors?" Monique asked.

"I haven't quite decided yet," Kyle responded.

As Monique is about to ask another question, in walks a 6'3" man with olive skin, thick black slightly wavy hair with a patch of grey in the front, a face that looks like it was chiseled by a master sculptor, and piercing green eyes. Wearing black khaki pants and a navy and white striped polo shirt, he approaches the ladies.

"Hello, I am here to see Miss DeBrow," the man said.

"I'm Miss DeBrow," Kyle responded.

"Good afternoon, I'm Patrick Richards. I'm here to discuss your infrastructure requirements," he said, extending his hand. Kyle quickly caught herself staring.

"Oh! I didn't realize you were schedule for today," Kyle exclaimed in surprise as she shakes his hand.

"Well, I may be about 30 minutes early but I have you on the calendar for today," looking on his phone to double check.

"I am so sorry Monique. Can you scan through this floor solo for a bit? I have to take Mr. Richards up to 35," Kyle asked.

"Of course. No problem, Monique responded.

"Okay, I am all yours," Kyle said, turning to Patrick. "Can we start on the 35th floor? That's where my, the Chief Creative Director, the Chief Financial Officer, some other offices, cubicles, as well as our large conference rooms are going to be."

"Sure. Whatever you'd like," Patrick responded smiling.

They walked out the hall and Kyle pushed the elevator button.

"I'm sorry about the mess. They are still working on the offices, as you can see," Kyle said, pointing to the plastic on the floor and blue painting tape covering the walls.

"So what's the deadline for completion of construction, if you don't mind my asking? Patrick asked as they stepped into the elevator.

"No, I don't mind at all. That's a great question. The answer is last month," Kyle said. "Unfortunately, the architect's plans and the final product of the 35th floor were drastically different, so I had a nice 'Come to Jesus' talk with the construction project manager, and we now have a completion date of about two and a half weeks," Kyle explained.

"Wow, that must suck," Patrick responded.

"Yeah, it does, because I have folks moving from New York, and no office to set them up in yet."

"Well, let's see how I can make your life a little less stressed and put a smile on your face. Stress gives you wrinkles, or at least that's what I hear," Patrick said as he laughs.

"So I hear," Kyle replied smiling. Is he flirting with me, Kyle thinks to herself.

"See? That's what we want. Okay, where would you like to start?" Patrick asks as they exit the elevator and walk into the suite...

As promised, the contractor completed the work at two week the deadline and Kyle and her entire team were finally able to settle in and move into the new office. She would see Patrick quite a bit while he and his team were working. He would pop into her office first thing in the morning, bring her a cup of tea with some fruit, and he'd always say, "Have a great day today, and don't forget to smile, boss lady."

Kyle would light up and smile every time. She would always struggle with thinking was he just being a nice guy or was he attempting to show her he was interested. So when it was getting close to Kyle's birthday, Bethany was running herself crazy helping finishing up a surprise party at the direction of Kyle's friends, of course. Kyle would have killed her had she known what she was up too, especially during work hours. All she could hear is, "The magazine comes first, everything else is last." As she was on the phone with the event planner, Patrick happened to walk by and overhear her conversation.

"Hey Bethany, is it the boss lady's birthday?" Patrick asked

"Oh yeah, it's this weekend, and I am trying to help with the surprise party planning," Bethany replied, looking overwhelmed.

"Do you know the exact date?"

"Oh yeah, I'm sorry, it's January 28th."

"Thanks," Patrick said and walks off.

"Hey, wait!" Bethany yelled.

"Yes, ma'am?" Patrick said, popping his head back into the office.

"Would you be interested in coming?" Bethany asked

"I wouldn't want to intrude on her personal time. Isn't it going to be for her close friends? Patrick inquired.

"Dude, you bring her breakfast almost every day and keep us all from being yelled at from her hungry outbursts. I think that certifies you as a friend," Bethany says smirking at him. "Plus there will be people from here going, including myself, so I think you're fine to be on the invite list."

"Okay, sure. Send me the information please," Patrick responded.

"I will email you the details," said Bethany.

"Email the details of what?" Kyle inquired as she walks out of her office, only having heard the tail end of the conversation.

"Oh, I have some small issues with my Adobe Pro and Patrick said to email him the exact issue so he can put a ticket in with the help desk for me," Bethany said, smoothly covering up the truth.

"Oh, okay," Kyle said. "So, what do you think of our new digs chief?" Kyle asked Patrick.

"It's really nice. I have never seen anything like it."

"Perfect! That is exactly what I was going for," Kyle said with a huge smile on her face, then turned to Bethany, "I must run out for a meeting with the creative director over at Delilah's. I will be back in about an hour and a half."

"Okay, I will text you if anything major arises while you're gone," Bethany responded. Kyle nodded and rushed out the door.

"Is it hard working for the boss lady?" Patrick asked

"Yes and no," Bethany said. "She is a great boss, very generous and thoughtful, but on the other hand she is highly demanding and task oriented. She knows what and how she wants things, so you have to be a strong person to work for her, because she will tell you if she doesn't like it and it may not be in the most candy-coated manner."

"I imagine that is why she is so successful."

"She's a bulldog when it comes to her business and she leaves zero room for error. She will fire you with no problem. However, she also will give you the shirt off her back if she likes you. I know from personal experience. My first year with her, I was so behind on my bills. I was so stressed. We had a long talk because she saw me in the parking lot crying. After a lot of pushing from her, I told her what was going on and she wrote me a check to pay my rent for 6 months to help me get caught up," Bethany said.

"Really? Wow, she's a hell of a person," Patrick said in amazement.

"Yes, she definitely is," Bethany confirmed.

"Okay, I will let you get back to work. Have a good day. I'll see you around," Patrick said.

"Okay, you have a good day, too," Bethany said.

Oh, one more question. I don't want to come to her party empty handed. What should I get her for her birthday? What does she like? Patrick asked.

"Perfume, her favorite is Chloe, scarves, and music. I always give her iTunes gift cards, perfume and a scarf or flowers" Bethany answered.

"Okay great, thanks," Patrick said and walked away.

"Hmm…he wants to buy her a gift. That's so thoughtful," Bethany said to herself.

****

Ting! Ting! Ting! Kyle's phone was buzzing repeatedly. She picked up her phone and looked at the time and who was texting her. Her phone read January 28th, 7:02am, along with a text from dad and Tangi. Kyle reads through all the messages.

Dad: Happy Birthday, baby girl! I love you and I am proud of you. Call me later. Love Dad.

Kyle: Thanks Dad! Love you too. I will come by a little later.

Next message:

Tangi: Hey birthday girl! We still doing dinner tonight, right?

Kyle: Yes ma'am, and please do not tell them it's my birthday. I hate when they come to the table and sing.

Tangi: I won't! I promise.

Kyle: Much appreciated! I have to stop by Studio 616 at like 5pm. Bethany said we have some last minute walk-throughs to go over for the special edition event. I will get out of there as early as possible, so I can meet you on time.

Tangi: Okay perfect! I wish you weren't going to work today, but I know you. The magazine first, everything else second! Try and enjoy your day.

Kyle: I will I have an appointment at the spa. Massage, facial, and some sort of sugar scrub and body wrap that Asia made for me at her place. So I will be glowing and relaxed. LOL!

Tangi: LOL! Nice!!! Enjoy and I'll see you later.

Kyle: Did I tell you I bought myself a Bday gift? Going to pick that up in about an hour.

Tangi: Not the Maserati???

Kyle: Yep!!! Hashtag, Happy birthday to me!!!! <3 <3 <3

Tangi: I ain't mad at you at all!! I'm happy for you! You work hard and deserve it! You will definitely enjoy your day today.

Kyle: Sure will! Thanks for the Bday wish Tan! I love you!

Tangi: Girl, of course. I love you too! See you later.

Kyle: Kissing emoji

****

While at the car dealership Kyle gets a text from Patrick.

Patrick: Good morning boss lady, can you meet me at your office really quickly? I have to reset your system. It should only take about 10 minutes.

Kyle: Okay I will be there in about 20 mins.

Patrick: Okay, thanks.

"Ms. DeBrow, your car is ready," the salesman said, handing her a pair of shiny new keys.

"Great!" Kyle said, walking to the front. She walks out the door and looks at her new car, pearl white with charcoal grey and white leather interior, custom black rims, and Pirelli tires. Kyle's face lights up.

"I'm going to burn the highway down in this," Kyle said to herself and got into the car and drove off, on her way back to the office.

Kyle pulled into the garage just as Patrick pulled up and parked a couple of spaces away from her.

"Hey boss lady. Nice ride! Is this new? I thought you had a Rang Rover .

"I did. I decided to get something new," Kyle answered.

"Did you not like the Rover?" Patrick asked as they walk to the elevator.

"No, I liked it. I just wanted something new," Kyle said.

"Oh, must be nice," Patrick said.

"So what floor do you need to start on?" Kyle asked.

"Oh, we can start on your suite in your office, then the others," Patrick responded.

Kyle unlocked the door and walked into her office.

"Oh my God! What the...? – she stopped in her tracks. What looked like 50 vases of pink and white peonies along with white and yellow roses flourishing all over her office. A blue Tiffany's box on her desk being the cherry on top.

"Isn't today the boss lady's birthday?" Patrick asked.

"Yes, today is my birthday. Hold on, did you do this? How did you know?" Kyle asked.

"I have my sources," Patrick said smiling.

"Thank you so much, Patrick I am at a loss of words. This is so nice!"

"Aren't you going to open the box?" Patrick asked. Kyle walks over to her desk, opened the Tiffany's box, and saw a beautiful set of engraved sterling silver pens that read FNBK.

"Patrick this was so nice of you! I cannot even imagine how to thank you," Kyle said almost in tears.

"Well, since you are always stealing my pens, I thought I'd get you your own. I like to be proactive, plus I wanted to do something nice for the prettiest lady I know," Patrick explained.

"I cannot believe this. Thank you very much!" Kyle said. "Is it okay if I give you a hug?

"Of course boss lady," he responded as he walked over to her and wrapped his arms around her waist. Kyle wrapped her arms around his neck and hugged him close, inhaling deep, taking in the smell of his cologne. Melting into his arms she closed her eyes, then catches herself.

Am I holding on too long? she started thinking. She released Patrick from her hold.

"Thank you so much again," Kyle said.

"No problem boss lady. It's my pleasure, Patrick replied.

"The question now is how did you get in here to do all of this?" Kyle asked as they walk out her office and towards the elevators.

"Now that part is a secret," Patrick said.

Kyle looked down at her watch, "Oh my goodness! I'm going to be late! I have to meet Bethany at the venue we are having our special edition event," Kyle exclaimed. "Patrick, thank you so much. Will you be at the office on Monday?" she asked.

"Unfortunately, no. We've finished setting up your in house IT department," he explained as they walk into the elevator.

"Oh, well do you think you will be free for lunch?"

"Absolutely, just let me know what time and where,"

"Perfect, I will see you then."

"Sounds like a plan," Patrick confirms.

They walked out into the parking garage together. Patrick gets into his SUV and Kyle gets into her pearly white Maserati. She waved at Patrick and pulled off.

Kyle called Bethany.

"Hey, I'm running home to change and I will be there right on time," Kyles said.

"Okay," Bethany answered. "I will see you shortly."

Kyle pulled up to her house and ran straight to her bedroom.

"Oh thank God!" she said, looking on the bed and seeing that she had already pulled her outfit for dinner out of the closet. She jumped in the shower, did her makeup and hair, sprayed a couple of spritzes of Chloe on, and got dressed.

She zoomed in her car and pulled into the parking lot at the venue, noticing tons of cars were already there.

"Oh wow! I hope we are not intruding on an event," Kyle said to herself.

Bethany walks out the door of the venue to meet Kyle outside.

"Hey, are we walking into an event in progress?" Kyle asked.

"Yes, but the event planner wanted you to see what the place looks like all gussied up and with people in it," Bethany explained. "Don't get your feathers all rustled up, okay? she reassured Kyle as they walked in.

"Happy birthday!!!"

A huge group of Kyle's friends and counterparts shouted in unison. Kyle is totally surprised and blown away. She looked at Bethany, smile at her, then walked toward all of her friends, hugging each person one by one. Bethany let out a sigh of relief and joined the rest of the party.

"I am going to kill you all!" Kyle yelled out, walking toward Evian, Asia, Tangi, Mike and Leslie, who all had their arms open for a group hug. "I cannot believe I didn't see this coming," Kyle said. "And you had me so fooled!" pointing at Tangi.

"Girl. you no I'm an actress. I act!" Tangi said, flipping her hair over her shoulder.

"I definitely won't argue that," Kyle said, smiling sarcastically.

"Well, enough of all this mushy gushy stuff, it's party time!" Asia said, walking toward the dance floor.

"Here we come, girl!" Evian said, grabbing Kyle and Tangi's hands, they walked toward the dance floor. As the girls were dancing, Kyle felt a tap on her shoulder. She turned around to see Patrick.

"Oh wow! You are good, I had no idea you would be here either!" Kyle said, dancing with a big smile.

"Excuse me, ladies. Can I steal the birthday girl away for a birthday dance? I promise I will return her safely to you," Patrick asked smiling at the girls, and gently took Kyle's hand.

The girls look at each other and then at Kyle.

"Of course you may," Tangi replied.

****

Kyle and Patrick had dated on and off for about 3 and a 1/2 years after her birthday surprises. At one point they would be doing great, having fun and supporting each other's endeavors. As soon as the discussions about where they were headed started, Patrick would often disappear. He and Kyle would stop speaking and then reconcile a few weeks later. When they finally thought that they had it all right and in a good place, probably halfway through year three, Patrick started having issues with Kyle's level of success. During one of their many 'conversations' at his house, Patrick told Kyle that dating someone like her was too much because he wasn't the 'be-in-the-spotlight' type of guy.

"I like people not knowing who I am or who I am dating," Patrick explained.

"What do you mean? You knew how successful I was from the very beginning and told me you were fine with it," said Kyle.

"I just want to be known for who I am not who I am dating. And as much as I love you and care about you, I do not want to be Mr. DeBrow," Patrick said.

"I am still confused. It's not like you are in the tabloids or the news," Kyle explains.

"Yes, you're right. But when we go out, people seem to address you and then me, or if I am out alone someone will sometimes ask about you before they even greet me."

"Oh, I see. Well, then I will not cause your life another minute of distraction," Kyle said, and quickly packs up her bags. "I do not want this to become a thing, so I acknowledge your feelings, but I do not have anything else to say," she said, and walked out the front door.

She refused to give him the satisfaction of seeing her cry. If he thinks he is going to see me breakdown, he can think again, Kyle thought, putting her bags in the car. She wiped the tears from her face and sped off down the street.

Back at home Kyle was a mess. She took off two weeks from work and did nothing but cry on the couch. The ladies would come over and try and cheer her up, but it never worked. Asia would sit with her and try and get her to meditate. Evian and Leslie would come over and try and give her the 'It wasn't you, it was him' speech. But what finally got her out the house, was Tangi's complaining.

"Kyle, I love you, but girl you have got to shake this shit off," Tangi said. "You have played Broken Record by Tamar so much that no one wants to come over here anymore. Your neighbors think you are on some kind of suicide watch. Is this what you want? To be in the papers? The great Kylisha DeBrow on suicide watch?" Tangi said. "Sitting at home crying, singing your woes and eating Godiva chocolate covered strawberries. Hair not done, wearing the same damn PJs, looking like who did it and why. What in the entire hell, girl?!

Get up, wash your face, take a shower, and let's go eat before I take a picture of you and post it on IG and Twitter with the #whenyoureonsuicidewatch my damn self!" Tangi warns.

All of the sudden, Kyle got up and said, "Girl, you wouldn't."

Tangi pulls out her phone.

"Okay, okay! I'm getting up," Kyle surrendered and walked to the shower.

Chapter 7

Being Partner....

"Good morning Jack," Evian says as she walks into the Partner's suite where Jack Hunter, a fellow partner is waiting on her in his office.

"Evian, I wanted to congratulate you officially this morning," Jack says.

"Thank you Jack," Evian responds.

"Evian, you have been the most successful VP Level Sports Manager we have had in years. The amount of business you have brought to this firm has been unprecedented. It didn't take much of a debate to make you a partner," Jack says. "We all agreed that you were the best choice."

"I truly appreciate that Jack. We have a great team and I do my best in ensuring that we stay the number one firm in the country," Evian says.

"And that is exactly why you were the best choice to become partner," Jack says.

"Jack, are you content with the agency as it is?" Evian asks.

"What do you mean? Jack responds.

"Well, I would really like to begin to focus on branching out and brainstorming on how to expand. Why should we limit our firm to only the sports industry? I think we can expand into the entertainment industry, especially since some of our biggest clients are more than just athletes," Evian says.

"You are absolutely right, Evian. We have been wanting to expand, but haven't had the right person to take that task on. Walk me through what you are thinking regarding to how we can begin the expansion," Jack inquires

"Well, I think for starters we need to develop an Entertainment Division, go through our current roster of agents and see who may be a good candidate for a promotion or transfer. I think the agents that can handle both deserve some sort of promotion and the ones that may be struggling in the Sports Division may be better served in the Entertainment Division," Evian explains.

"However, I want to be clear that this will not be an easy selection process because we need strong, hungry, and motivated agents, not entitled ones," Evian continues. "We need to vet the current agents thoroughly.

A little healthy competition can't hurt, we will give folks a chance to earn a spot before we start opening up spots to external agents. I already have some agents with a great roster that are just waiting to come on board, as well as a couple of potential clients who were waiting for me to either leave and start my own firm or make partner and drop the expansion bug in your ear," Evian says smiling.

"That all sounds great, but also very time consuming. Can you handle spearheading this project?" Jack asks.

"Absolutely," Evian responds confidently. "I think it would be a good idea to announce the potential expansion at the morning meeting, so we can hear from the other agents. They may have ideas or potential clients we are unaware of," Evian recommends. "Now, of course this means some people will have to go. We can't afford to have under-performers if we are going to take on such a big project."

"I agree 100%," Jack responds. "While we are on the subject of under-performers, let's talk about Jake. To be totally transparent, I have my concerns regarding his ability to close lately. He has not signed on anyone new this entire quarter. "I'm not sure if he is just having a rough patch, if he's upset about something, perhaps the fact that he didn't qualify for partner, or if he's just cruising because his parents and I are very close friends and he believes he is untouchable because they were able to get him in the door."

"We haven't gotten rid of him because when he first got hired he was driven and signed some really big clients. Those same clients are also unhappy with him and are looking to move on from what I have been hearing," Evian says.

"I've heard the same, but was hoping it was a rumor," Jack confesses.

"I think we, meaning all the partners, need to have a serious discussion with him regarding his performance, and maybe this new division will get him excited again," Evian says.

"I agree. I will let you take the lead on this," Jack says.

"Let's attack this today. We can ask that he stays when everyone else leaves after the morning meeting, since we will all be there. We can kill two birds with one stone," Evian says.

"Sounds good. Let's bring Phillip up to speed now," Jack says.

"Okay, Evian" says as they walk out of Jack's office.

Evian walks into the conference room with several legal pads, folders, and her iPad in her hands. She sits her iPad and one of the folders down at the head of the table. The other partners walk in behind her and take their seats around the table. The meeting begins.

"Good Morning everyone, I am sure by now you have heard the great news," says Phillip Hoffman, one of the partners. "Evian has accepted our offer for partner. Please join me in congratulating and welcoming her into this new role."

Everyone around the table applauds and offers their congratulations.

"Evian has work very hard and has been one of the major reasons our firm has been as successful as it has. I think I speak for the rest of the partners when I say it is an honor and a privilege to have her with us," Phillip continues. I am not going to take up too much time, because I know Evian has a number of items to go over with you all, but I do want you all to know there are some great things happening here, and we will need all of you to get us to where we are going. Evian the floor is yours."

"Thank you so much Philip and Jack for the vote of confidence in me. Thank you for this partnership, and most importantly, thank each and every one of you all in this room. We have all worked very hard to make this agency what it is today, so for that you all deserve a round of applause," Evian says as she claps her hands and looks around the room at the group of men and women sitting around the conference table.

Everyone joins in and applauses.

"That's right, you all deserve it," Evian says. "Now let's get down to business," she says smiling. "Effective today we will have daily huddles first thing in the morning."

She passes folders and pads around the table for everyone to have their own.

"During these huddles, we will be discussing who is signing on, who you are already working with, and who are you potentially thinking about going after. I have a wealth of knowledge that has helped me close several deals with some of the most influential athletes this agency has ever seen, and I am not one to keep the secrets all to myself. Feel free to use me as a resource when you are experiencing difficulty or are just not sure what angle you want to take. I also want to know who your next potential clients are, your strategy for closing the deal with them, and finally, where your sights are pointed next."

Evian gives each person around the table eye contact and smiles, showing that she cares – cueing her Mama Bear status. All the team members around the table smile back and are engaged in what she is saying.

"This is your meeting, so I want you to feel free to discuss matters you determine are pressing or would like your team's feedback on," Evian emphasizes. "Each day, one of you will facilitate the meeting. I have no plans of sitting here doing all the talking every day. This is not college and I am not here to lecture you. Again, this is your meeting. I want to hear from you all. I have expectations of you all, as I am sure you all have expectations of me. Today, that is exactly what we are going to discuss."

She walks to the white board behind her.

Let's get down to it. I am sure this goes without saying, but I will say it for arguments sake, our expectation of you all is to close deals, pointblank period," she says as she writes expectations, on the white board.

"Now my personal expectations of you all are that you will be honest, ethical, and respectful of our clients and most importantly, each other. The only person who can change the direction of a potential client is myself and one of the other partners. Which means no one is to steal anyone else's client under any circumstances. That type of behavior is not reflective of the mission of our agency," she states clearly and concisely, with a hint of authority. "I also have a big announcement to make."

Evian gears up for what she hopes will be something accepted and well received by everyone.

"We will be expanding the agency and adding an Entertainment Division," Evian says. The look of excitement starts to show around the room.

"We would like to recruit from within, and we will also need someone to run the division as well. No, you will not have to give up your current roster in order to be considered, in case you were wondering," she clarifies before anyone objects.

"For some, this will be an opportunity for advancement, and for others it will be an opportunity to transfer to a better fitting role," Evian explains.

"Can you explain what you mean by that?" a man asks from the table.

"Of course, Evian responds, happy that someone finally said something. "Some folks will be promoted since they will be handling both clients on the sports side and the entertainment side. Others who would like to make a change and transfer to the Entertainment Division, this is their opportunity," Evian explains.

Seeing some members smiling after she said her last statement made Evian feel like a million bucks. It confirmed her confidence that this is the direction to go.

"Those of you who are interested, please set up a meeting with me via Todd so we can discuss in what capacity you would like to be considered. Once we have decided who will go where I will meet with the candidate we select to run the division on a weekly basis to go over what we need to do to get this division off and running."

And now for the final point.

"We would like to have the division running by the fall, which means we don't have much room for dilly dallying, so whoever assumes this will have a lot of work on their hands."

"Will you be accepting appointments immediately?" a woman asked.

"Absolutely," Evian says. "I hope you all are excited as we are to begin this new venture," Evian concludes. "Okay, I will let you guys get to the rest of your day and I look forward to hearing more of what you all have going on and how I can assist in making it happen."

As everyone started exiting the conference room, Jake approaches Jack and asks if he can speak with him privately.

"I am so glad you asked, because we actually wanted to meet with you briefly," Jack responds.

"Phil and I will allow you two to chat, and we will return in about 15 or 20 minutes," Evian says looking at Jake and Jack.

"Yes, that sounds good," Jack responds.

Phil and Evian exit the conference room.

"Are you a gambler?" Phil asks Evian as they walk towards the partners suite

"I am. Why? Evian responds with an inquisitive grin.

"I bet you $100 he is in there asking to run the Entertainment Division," Phil says with his hand out.

"I will take that bet. There is no way he has the balls to ask that, knowing how shaky his performance has been," Evian says, grabbing Phil's hand to shake.

Phil winks at Evian and they both walk into their offices.

"So, what's on your mind Jake?" Jack asks.

"Well, I wanted to talk to you about the Entertainment Division," Jake says.

"Okay," Jack responds.

"Well, I have been thinking that I would be a good candidate to run that division," Jake says.

"Well, that is actually Evian's brainchild, so the best person to discuss this with is going to be her," Jack says.

"Not a problem. I will schedule a time to meet with her ASAP," Jake says with a look of disappointment on his face.

"Pardon me for a moment Jake. I am going to go find Phil and Evian and let them know you are ready to meet with all of us," Jack says.

"Jack, do you have any idea what this meeting is about?" Jake asks

"I do, but I would rather all the partners be present for the discussion. Don't worry, you're not being fired," Jack reassures Jake.

Jake sits in the conference room, checking emails on his phone and scrolling through Instagram when Jack, Evian and Phil walk in.

"So, Jack tells me that you are interested in being considered for the Entertainment

Division Department Head position," Evian tells Jake.

"Yes, I am," Jake says confidently.

"Well, let's discuss that a little. How do you think you have been performing lately?" Evian asks.

"Why? Do you have some concerns with my performance? Jake asked.

"No need to get defensive Jake. Evian speaks for all of us," Phil says.

Jake sits up straight in his chair, "Well, overall I think I've been doing well. I had a rough patch last quarter due to some issues that were no fault of mine, but my numbers have been steady and I haven't lost one client since I have been with the firm," Jake says.

"I know you haven't lost any clients, but some of the contracts have either fell through the cracks or came very close to falling through, to the point where others had to step in to assist in closing the deals," Evian states. "Based on the fact that one of those mishaps caused us to miss out on a multimillion-dollar deal because you felt the original offer was 'too low and not worth your client's time', we will have to put you on a temporary probation.

Jakes face fell and gave a look of disbelief.

"Now before you get too upset," Phil continued, "this will not affect your ability to apply or interview for the Entertainment Head position. We have a lot of work to do, and won't be holding interviews for quite some time, as logistically there are some things that need to be thought through and planned out."

"I understand," Jake says, holding in his anger.

"So the timeline is 90 days. We will discuss the performance improvement plan with you when we get all the paperwork completed with HR. Do you have any questions for us? Evian asks.

"No. None," Jake says as he gets up from the table.

"Okay. Should you think of anything please feel free to come speak with any of us," Phil says.

Jake walks out the room.

"Well that went better than expected," Jack says.

"Drinks are on Evian after work," Phil says smiling.

"You got it. Shall we say 6:30?" Evian says smiling, understanding that she lost the bet with Phil.

"Sounds good to me," Jack says.

"I'll see you there," Phil says as he holds the door open for Evian and Jack to walk out.

"Oh yeah, Evian I had my assistant email you your office decor budget. You may want to get started on that, cause once you start turning the new division wheel you won't have time for much else," Jack says smiling.

"Speaking of assistants, are you taking Todd with you or leaving him for whomever fills your spot and hiring someone else?" Phil asks.

"I am pretty sure he is coming with me. I wouldn't feel right giving someone else that job," Evian says.

"Okay, make sure you have HR do the necessary paperwork to have him transferred and then he can go ahead and move to our suite."

"I'm on it," she confirms.

Next step, send the ladies a text to group chat.

Evian: Guess what? I got the green light on my expansion proposal! happy face emoji

Kyle: That's amazing news!!

Asia: Congratulations! as the screen explodes with a confetti GIF.

Leslie: You better work girl!!!! I am so happy for you!

Tangi: That's what's up! Congrats diva!!!

Evian: Les, I may need you and Mike to help with this and some other irons I have in the fire.

Asia: For a woman in such a male-dominated industry you are killing the game luv. I am proud of you! Make sure you schedule a weekly meditation. Biggie said it best: More money more problems...LOL! crying laughing emoji

Leslie: You know we got you, just tell us what you need.

Kyle: How did your talk go with the spoiled brat???

Tangi: I was just about to ask the same question...you know we hate him!!! Lol

Evian: It started off rocky, and I am sure he is a little pissed we put him on probation. But either he will rise to the occasion and get better or he will crash and burn.

Asia: Spoken like a true Boss!!

Leslie: I concur!

Kyle: That's my girl!!!

Tangi: OMG, I bet he is in his office having a silent fit...LOL! Good!!!

Evian: LMAO you are crazy!!!

Evian: Oh yeah, they gave me an amazing office décor budget. Kyle can you put me in touch with your interior decorator?

Tangi: Now that is what the hell I am talking about!!!!

Kyle: LMAO! crying emoji Of course girl, I will text you her info.

Evian: Thanks girl! Okay ladies, I have to get back to work. I love you all! Kisses

Kyle: Love you more!

Asia: Not more than me!!!

Tangi: Love you to the moon and back!

Leslie: With all that love you don't need mine, JK. Love you in infinite amounts, doll!

****

Jake sends a text while sitting in his office.

Jake: That bitch had the nerve to insinuate that I do not work hard. Who the fuck does she think she is?! And they put me on probation! I know it was all her idea.

Bro: Dude, relax! You said you have a plan, so just focus on that and not on the she-devil.

Jake: You're right. I will cross that bridge when I have to. TTYL

Bro: Okay.

Chapter 8

Fashion and friends just don't mix...

"Good morning, Bethany," Kyle says as she walks into the office.

"Happy Monday, boss lady. Someone looks like they had a restful weekend," Bethany observes, smiling from ear to ear and passing a cup of tea to Kyle.

"Yes, I actually relaxed by the pool all weekend with the girls. I didn't even check my email until Sunday," Kyle says proudly.

"That's great to hear! So, we are all set for Shalon's shoot and interview. It's all scheduled for Wednesday."

"Perfect!" Kyle responds. "I still have some loose ends to tie up with next month's issue, so I will be in the office with the door closed for most of the day. If you need me just come on in. Do not, I repeat, do not let anyone in my office to bother me. I need to focus," Kyle says.

"No problem. I will just tell people you are on conference calls and aren't available," Bethany replies.

"Okay, thank you. Ugh, I just remembered I need an outfit for the Tom ford event tonight. I may need you to give Elina's Boutique a call and see if Tiffany can pull some looks for me and have them sent over," Kyle says.

"Not a problem. I will call Tiffany, and then get with Monica and Lisa from the Beauty Department and have them come here by 3ish to get started on your hair and makeup," Bethany says.

"Great, thank you," Kyle responds. She closes her office door and gets down to work. While sifting through articles and storyboards, Kyle's phone starts to light up and buzz. It's a text from Asia.

Asia: Hey Kyle, how's your day going?

Kyle: Busy as shit! Stressed emoji.

Asia: Want to do dinner after work?

Kyle: I can't, I have that Tom Ford event. Tan is coming with me. I invited her last week. Wait, she is still going, right?

Asia: OMG that's tonight! I didn't even remember. Yes, she is going. That must be why she went to the hair salon early this morning. I hope you two have fun!

Kyle: I am honestly way too busy getting last minute things finished for next month's issue. I had to have several articles rewritten and several shoots redone. They were simply horrendous. But I cannot not go, so I will get dressed, smile and see what he has coming for the Fall. Then run back to the office to finish up. So unfortunately, fun is last on my list today.

Asia: I'm so sorry things are so stressful. Do you need me to send someone over for a short meditation break?

Kyle: No thanks, but thank you for the offer. I am way too busy. Kisses emoji.

Asia: Okay, I won't keep you. Try and have a good day. Love you!

Kyle: I love you too. Heart emoji.

Kyle picks up the phone to call Bethany.

"Bethany, I know I said not to let anyone in here, but could you call the Arts Department and tell them I need an emergency meeting to walk through this markup they sent me?" Kyle asks.

"Sure no problem," Bethany responds.

****

Tangi sits in the salon chair as her stylist finishes up her hair.

"So why the need for such an early morning appointment Tan?" the stylist asks.

"Oh, I'm going to a Tom Ford event and I still need to put an outfit together and see a few of my clients all before 4pm. Then I have to run to Kyle's office in time to get my makeup done. Speaking of which, I need to text her and let her know I am coming there and will ride with her to the event."

"I am not trying to get in your business, but isn't that a bit last minute mama? the stylist asks.

"Girl, no!" Tangi says excitedly. "Me and Kyle are close, she won't mind at all. Trust me."

"It must be nice. I wish I had friends like that," the stylist says. "Okay mama, you are all done," turning Tangi's chair towards the mirror.

"Thanks girl, it looks good. Let me get on out of here," Tangi says as she walks towards the reception area to pay.

"Have fun girl!" the stylist responds.

Tangi gets in her car and texts Kyle.

Tangi: Hey Kyle, I will be over at your office around 3 to get my makeup done and get dressed so I can ride with you over to the venue.

Let me get over to my first client before she has a fit. She's only been texting me all morning, Tangi thinks to herself.

"Maybe I should just give her a call," Tangi says to herself. "Call Helena!" Tangi yells in her car.

"Calling Helena" the car responds in a robotic voice. Helena is one of Tangi's wealthiest clients, one of LA's "grand socialites"

"Hey Helena," Tangi says.

"Tangi, where have you been? I have been texting you all morning. We had a 10am meeting," Helena says.

"I know, I am so sorry. I ran a bit over in my last appointment, but I am on my way," Tangi replies.

"A text to let me know would have helped. I have already called my backup. She is here and we have already chosen which outfit I am going to wear this evening," Helena says. "I don't know what's going on with you darling, but you have been a little flakey lately. But we can chat more about that at the event tonight. You are still going to be there, yes?" Helena asks.

"Yes, I will be there," Tangi replies.

"Good. Stop by my table and we can chat. I have to go darling. I will see you there.

Goodbye," Helena says and disconnects from the call.

"She's being a bit of a drama queen today," Tangi says to herself. "Hmm…Kyle didn't text be back, she must be away from her phone." Well, that gives me more time to go pick out my outfit and run a couple more errands.

****

"I am going to need this shoot redone ASAP, and why was the location changed without someone talking with me first? Kyle asks the group from the Arts Department sitting in her office, all four start jotting notes down in their notepads. No one answers.

"Doesn't matter change it back, redo the shoot, and have the proofs to me by Thursday close of business.

"Yes, Ms. DeBrow," the group says and walks out of her office.

Just as they are walking out, Dina from Elina's Boutique walks in with several garment bags in hand and her assistant with shoe boxes in tow.

"Hey Kyle, you ready for me?" Dina asks.

"Oh my god, I almost forgot all about the event! Yes, D, I'm ready. Please excuse my bitchy attitude, I promise it is not for you. Please tell me you have something that will make me look better than I feel, because right now, I am ready to just go home and get in bed," Kyle confesses.

"Oh no, you will not be going to bed on my watch! Don't do that," Dina says laughing. "Okay, so are you feeling like a dress, pants, shorts? I brought it all!"

"Hmm…" Kyle says with her right index finger on her bottom lip. "You choose, I am too exhausted to even think. I trust you," she surrenders throwing her hands up in the air.

"I think we will show off those sexy long legs and go with some black sequin shorts, an orange, grey, and black floral print off the shoulder shear blouse, gold bracelet, and these black and white striped Louboutin's."

Dina pulls the pieces out of their garment bags and lays them on the loveseat together, putting the stilettos on the coffee table.

"That was quick!" Kyle says smiling.

"Well, I was thinking of looks for you on the way here, and was hoping you'd let me pick for you," Dina says handing Kyle the hangers and shoe box. "Let's see it on and see if it looks how I picture it in my head. Do you need us to step out so you can change? Dina asks.

"Girl no we are all women in this room," Kyle says as she undresses and puts on the shorts first.

"Okay, what do you think?" Dina asks as she helps Kyle get her top on.

"I like it a lot. What should I do with my hair?"

"Tell whoever is doing your hair to give you a sleek ponytail, so everyone can see your face and shoulders," Dina says.

"This definitely is it. I love this, D! Charge it to my account," Kyle says with excitement.

"You got it! Don't forget what I said about the hair," Dina says, grabbing the rest of the garment bags and leaves with her assistant.

"I won't, and thanks D!" Kyle says.

Like a revolving door, the next batch enters the office.

"You are just in time," Kyle says as two members of the beauty department come to do her hair and makeup.

"Okay, for hair we can keep it simple with a sleek ponytail to the back. And makeup, I'm your canvas just do not make me look like a circus clown," Kyle laughs.

"I think we will keep it simple but edgy," the hairstylist Monica, says winking at Kyle. "We will do a reversed smokey eye and keep the rest of your face as natural as possible. I won't go all JLo glow on you," Lisa, the makeup artist says.

"The JLo glow is beautiful, but I thank you, I am not feeling like being too glowy today," Kyle replies.

A few minutes pass, Tangi appears, walking into the suite and down the hall. Just as she is about to open the door to Kyle's office she hears, "Good afternoon Ms. Charles," Bethany says as she stops her.

"Hey Bethany, I'm Kyle's guest for the Tom Ford event. I was just going in to see if her team has time to do my makeup before we leave together," Tangi says nonchalantly.

"Please have a seat Ms. Charles, and I will see if she is available."

Tangi gives her a confused look, but walks over to the sofa outside of Kyle's office and sits down. Bethany knocks and walks into Kyle's office.

"Tangi is here. She said something about getting her makeup done," Bethany says.

"Please tell Tangi that the team and I are finishing up and they will not have time to do her makeup, but she is welcome to head to the

Beauty Department and get samples to do her own makeup," Kyle says rolling her eyes.

"Will do," Bethany responds, leaving the office and updates Tangi.

"Ms. Charles, Ms. DeBrow said that hair and makeup will not have time to fit you in, but you are more than welcome to go down to the Beauty Department and sit at one of the stations to do your own makeup. The stations are fully stocked with everything you should need."

"But aren't they in there with her now? Tangi asks.

"Yes, they are. However, they are still assisting Ms. DeBrow, so I am not sure they will have time to finish up with her and start and finish your makeup in enough time for you all to head out. You know Ms. DeBrow will not want to be late for the event," Bethany says shrugging her shoulders.

"Yeah, you're right. She is a crazy person when it comes to punctuality. Okay, I will run downstairs. Tell her I will be back up 'on time'," Tangi says making quotation mark gestures with her fingers.

Bethany smiles, "Will do."

Bethany knocks and walks back in Kyle's office.

"Ms. DeBrow, Ms. Charles has gone down to the Beauty Department and said she will make sure she comes back up on time. Oh wow! You look amazing," Bethany says.

Kyle smiles, "Thank you so much. I was nervous cause I haven't been able to look in the mirror yet."

"I think you will be very pleased with the whole ensemble. You look like you should be downstairs participating in a shoot," Bethany says.

"You are too sweet. Thank you, Bethany."

"Okay, well I will leave you alone, and get back to– before she can finish Kyle interrupts her.

"You can go ahead and go home for the day if you want. I have kept you hostage long enough," Kyle says.

"Are you sure?" Bethany asks.

"Yes, I am positive. Go home," Kyle says smiling.

"Okay, thanks! Have fun and do not let anyone kill your vibe," Bethany says walking out the door.

"Okay, what do you think?" Monica asks handing Kyle a large portrait mirror.

"Oh wow! I love it. I love my hair and my makeup, is perfect, you guys are so freaking amazing!!! I am so lucky to have you," Kyle says.

As Lisa and Monica are walking out, Tangi struts in.

"Hey girl! Oh my gawd, you look amazing! Tangi says."That is the face beat I needed."

"Your makeup looks beautiful Tan, what are you talking about?" Kyle responds as they walk towards the elevators. "I love that jumpsuit, is that one of your designs?" Kyle asks pushing the elevator button to go downstairs.

"Why thank you Madame. Yes, this is one of mine," Tan says in a French accent doing a quick twirl in her black and yellow jumpsuit with zebra print heels. They both break out into laughter.

"So girl, you ready for this event? It will be a good opportunity for you to generate some buzz for your line," Kyle says as they step out of the elevator and out of the building to get into the private car waiting for them.

"Where to Ms. DeBrow?" the driver asks.

"Oh, I apologize. I thought I texted you the address. I will send it now," Kyle says pulling her phone from her purse and forwards the address in lightspeed.

"Got it, thank you," the driver says.

"Sorry Tan, as I was saying there will be tons of fashion media there so hopefully you can snag an interview on the side somewhere. I can reach out and put a bug in some of the folk's ears to go have a chat with you once the event is nearing the end too," Kyle says.

"That would be great! I am so lucky to have you, Kyle. You have been such a great friend to me," Tangi says. "I wanted to ask you how you felt about featuring my line in next month's issue?" Tangi asks.

"Hmm...I think I still may be able to get you into the Cutting Edge of Style section. I can have someone come to your studio later this week and take some photos, and have one of our writers do a short interview," Kyle responds.

"Wait, doesn't that section mostly feature up and coming stylists? Or it is for ones that are in high demand? Tangi asks.

"Yes, you are in high demand, and you can let folks know what's up and coming, giving them a peek at what you have going on," Kyle explains.

"I don't want to be featured in the style section," Tangi says sharply.

Kyle looks over at her, shocked and slightly confused.

"Well what section were you asking me for a write up in?" Kyle asks.

"What's Hot in Fashion," Tangi says in a matter-of-fact tone.

"That is absolutely not possible. And why would you think that that would be an option?" Kyle asks. "Apart from the cover story, it's one of the major articles for every issue. Do you know how much preparation goes into the What's Hot in Fashion article? Kyle asks.

"Girl, it isn't that deep. Have someone come over to my studio, just like you would have them meet with any other featured designer for the style section," Tangi says.

"Wait, what?!!" Kyle yells, catches herself, and whispers, "Are you fucking kidding me Tan?!" How dare you! "Let me give you a little bit of a lesson on how featured designers are selected in the event you do not know!" Kyle exclaims in a low yet whispered down tone. "First of all, you have to already have a line that is: (A) Generating revenue, and lots of it; (B) People are talking about it nonstop; and (C) You then have to send us a look book and schedule a viewing for our approval. I don't just blindfold myself and spin around to pick a designer like pin the tail on the goddamn donkey!" Kyle says. I can offer you the style section. And that my dear, is the best I can do. You can take it or leave it," Kyle says swiping her hands up and down together as a sign of being done with this conversation.

"I am going to leave it. And let me go on the record with saying that you didn't have any problem with helping Asia. You wrote up a whole one-page story on her and Zen Spas of Life and Wellness. New Year and a Beautiful New You is what you called it. And after that article, their business tripled and Asia had to go out of town constantly for months to help open new sites, 4 to be exact! Not to mention she got a crazy bonus," Tangi remarks.

The whole time Tangi was on her rant, Kyle was on her phone, texting the driver to pull over. She would catch a Lyft for the rest of the way, and to make sure Tangi arrived to the venue safely and was also returned home after the event.

"I cannot believe you," Kyle starts. You are so entitled and ungrateful. You haven't changed one bit from the girl that was too good to work at Neiman's. You lack humility and you believe things are supposed to just happen for you because what, you're cute, you're stylish, you have some famous clients? Girl wake up! As the car comes to a stop and Kyle gets out the car, she states, "For your information, I didn't cherry pick Asia or the Spa, one of my columnists did due to the buzz the Spa had created on their own! What I am not going to do is go back and forth about this. Here's your invite." Kyle lays Tangi's event invitation on the seat next to Tangi.

"I will see you at the venue, but this discussion is over!"Kyle says and slams the door, walking to the Lyft in a huff.

"Who the hell does she think she is talking to?! I should tell her where she can stick this damn invite," Tangi says to herself, but quickly snaps out of her anger, knowing she needs the opportunity to get the word out about her up and coming launch.

When Tangi first walks into the venue she runs into some of her clients. She feels a tap on her shoulder and turns around.

"Oh Helena! How are you?" Tangi asks looking her outfit up and down, thinking, I could have done a much better job.

"Tangi! Darling, you look stunning," Helena says.

"So do you," Tangi replies half-heartedly.

"Come, let's get a glass of champagne and have a little girl talk before the event begins," Helena says.

"Okay, Tangi," says as they walk towards the bar.

"What 's been going on with you darling? You have been missing in action these last couple of months. And when you do show up, it's normally late," Helena asks.

"I know I have been late a few times. I have been very busy with my new line and getting a studio for viewings, but I honestly do not know what you mean. I wouldn't consider that as me being MIA," Tangi explains.

"Darling, I have been with you from the very beginning. I was one of, if not your first client. You have always been very accessible and responsive, as well as punctual. But lately, all three of those things have been fading into the wind," Helena says gesturing her hand in a floating motion towards the sky. I do not want to, but I think I am going to have to hire someone to take your place," Helena says.

"With all due respect, Helena, I have worked very hard for you and I do not feel like my showing up late a few times should result in you firing me," Tangi says noticeably upset.

"Darling, if it were you only being late we wouldn't be having this discussion. You have changed, and it seems as if your clients are no longer your priority, and that's okay. I understand and support what you are doing, and as a matter of fact I will be the first one to make a purchase once your line is ready and available, but I really do need someone who has the time and desire to work with me, and clearly you do not," Helena says.

"If you feel like that is what you have to do, then I understand, but I wish you'd reconsider," Tangi says.

"Oh! There's Kylisha. She looks amazing. I would kill to have her legs," Helena says.

Kyle walks into the venue and notices Helena and Tangi talking on the terrace. She takes a deep breath, smiles and poses for the photographers at the entry of the event. Helena walks over to her.

"Kyle, you look ravishing."

"Helena! Oh my, it is good to see you. You look stunning. Tangi did and incredible job," Kyle says.

"Well, I will let Brittney know how well she did," Helena responds.

"How long have you been here? Did I miss anything? Kyle asks, purposely not unpacking Helena's response that it wasn't Tangi who dressed her.

"Oh I have only been here maybe 30 minutes, and the only thing you've missed are the hors d'oeuvres.

The room suddenly goes black.

"Oh! We'd better get to our table," Kyle whispers to Helena.

"That's if we can find it," Helena responds.

Strobe light start flickering and laser lights begin shooting all over the room. A spotlight hits the Emcee.

"Hello beautiful people! Let the fun begin!" he says into the microphone.

The show commences.

Chapter 9

Stuck in the middle...

Leslie comes out of the bedroom, hair in a low ponytail with her signature middle part, dressed in a fitted carnation pink sheath dress, heather grey suede pumps and a charcoal grey cardigan. She walks into the kitchen, wraps an apron around her waist and grabs the bag of bagels out of the cupboard. She starts the coffee maker for Mike, and puts the kettle on the stove for her tea.

"Mike!" Leslie yells from the kitchen. She walks closer to the bedroom door

"Sweetie, do you want a bagel with your coffee?"

"Mike walks to the bedroom doorway with a towel wrapped around his waist, little beads of water dropping down his dark chocolate skin. He smiles with his beautiful white teeth and deep dimples showing.

"Yes babe. Thank you. I have an early meeting, and will most likely miss lunch or have a late lunch, so this will be my nourishment," Mike responds, drying off his washboard stomach.

Leslie laughs.

"Heaven forbid you drop dead from malnourishment," she says sarcastically and laughing.

"I've had to fend for myself for the last couple of weeks, since my wife has abandoned me for work," Mike says shrugging his shoulders.

"You're absolutely right. Want me to make it up to you?" Leslie asks scanning Mikes body.

"Alright now. Don't play with me. Don't sign a check your ass can't cash," Mike responds.

Leslie laughs, "I can't recall a check I signed that couldn't be cashed."

"Now, you know I have to go, but I will be looking to cash your check later this evening," Mike says smiling.

"Oh, not a problem. I have some big plans for you this weekend, Mr. McCall," Leslie responds.

"Is that right? Well I am looking forward to the weekend Mrs. McCall," Mike says.

"Go get yourself dressed, I will get your coffee and bagel ready." Leslie says as she kisses Mike softly on his lips.

Mike smiles and shakes his head and walks back into the bedroom.

Mike finally walks out of the room fully dressed in a grey three-piece suit, with a lavender dress shirt, deep purple tie and tan belt and tan shoes.

"Look at you Mr. McCall. You look very handsome sir," Leslie says as she hands him a travel mug and a plate with a bagel on it.

"Why thank you my kind lady. You don't look to shabby either."

Mike takes a couple of bites from his bagel, kisses Leslie on the cheek, and playfully smacks her ass.

"Good day my lovely wife," Mike says and walks out the door.

"Bye my love," Leslie responds.

While in the car Mike calls Kyle.

"Why are you calling me? You better be on your way over here," Kyle says.

"Calm down drama queen. Leslie is on her way to you shortly. She is taking my place for today's meeting. I have another meeting to attend this morning," Mike says.

"Oh okay," Kyle says.

"So is that what you were calling for? To update me on your absence?" Kyle asks.

"Yes and no," Mike responds. I think Les might be pregnant," Mike says.

Trying to sound neutral, Kyle asks, "What makes you say that?"

"First of all, her breasts are huge. We have been fucking like rabbits, and every time I turn around she is jumping on me. She's always eating, and we both know Les eats like she's a model, afraid to gain weight."

"I don't want to talk you out of anything, but do not get your hopes up Mike. She could be stressed. Women eat their feelings sometimes," Kyle explains. "And for the sex, she might just miss her husband. You two have been fighting a lot lately."

Kyle hated to make him second guess his gut, but being that the last conversation she had with Leslie, she wasn't sure what Leslie had decided to do. She couldn't let him get his hopes up just to be wrong. She was cringing in her seat and her stomach was flipping.

"I just do not want you to get all excited to be let down, but I hope I am wrong and you are on your way to the Daddy-to-be club," Kyle says trying to sound optimistic.

"I hear you Kyle. I swear I do, but I am excited as hell at the possibility of her being pregnant and me being a father," Mike confesses. "If she is pregnant and agrees, will you be the babies Godmother?" Mike asks.

Kyle literally almost chokes on her tea attempting to answer the question with the thought that she may be right and Leslie may be possibly aborting the baby.

"Oh! Of course I will!" Kyle responds.

"Sooo," Mike says.

"Sooo what?" Kyle asks.

"Are you going to tell me what happened between you and Tan? I heard about the fight you two had," Mike asks.

"It was hardly a fight. I wouldn't even classify it as an argument," Kyle says. "She had the audacity to ask me to feature her in the What's Hot in Fashion article, you know the one that takes the entire month to get together? I offered her the Cutting Edge of Style section and she went to say no as if I offered her a pile of shit on a platter." She was so dismissive and nonchalant about our writing process and how we pick and put together our featured designers," Kyle begins to yell in frustration. "Wait, I'm sorry, I am not mad at you. I just get so pissed when I think of that conversation," Kyle says.

"It's okay. I understand, Tan can be a little entitled sometimes, but…"

"Mike, there is no but. Right is right and wrong is wrong," Kyle interrupts.

"I know, I know, but you know how she is. We all do," Mike says.

"Yeah, and you all always give her a pass, like when she asked you and Leslie to work on the contract with the distributer, and then last minute pulled out without telling you, and had you two sitting at a meeting that wasn't happening," Kyle says. "And then I look like the bad guy cause I call her out on her crap and hold her accountable." "I love Tan. I have always been in her corner. But this, this is just my breaking point with her.

I do not give her a pass. I was clear to her that I will never represent her again. Les is nicer than me," Mike says in a matter of fact tone. "She called Les on some weird 4 way call with the rest of the girls and complained about you abandoning her and yelling at her and being unreasonable and not a good friend," he says.

"Well she can keep that same energy the next time she sees me and for damn sure the next time she needs a favor," Kyle says. "Moving forward, I do not want to talk about

Tan. Who is this client that you are meeting with today? Are they new?" Kyle asks.

"No, actually it is with Evian and her Partners to discuss their expansion," Mike responds.

"I am so happy for Evian. She is really doing her thing. I remember her and her dad used to go to every sporting event," Kyle says.

"I know, she is amazing when it comes to sports management. I have seen her in action with clients, she's like the athlete whisperer," Mike says laughing.

"Yeah, she is," Kyle responds. "Well, have a good meeting and tell her hello for me," Kyle says.

"Okay, don't you drive my beautiful wife too crazy. I know how you do," Mike says.

"Bye Mike," Kyle says.

"Later," Mike says and ends the call.

Kyle drinks the rest of her tea and takes a moment to relax in her office before Leslie arrives.

"Good morning, Mrs. McCall. Ms. DeBrow is in the large conference room waiting for you," Bethany says to Leslie as she walks in.

"Good morning Bethany, how are you today?" Leslie asks.

"I am well, thank you. And yourself?" Bethany replies.

"I am good, thank you," Leslie says as she walks in the large conference room.

"Good morning, Les. I need to talk to you before everyone gets here. Have you spoken to Mike about– Before Kyle can complete her sentence Leslie falls to the floor.

"Oh my God!!! Kyle says running over to Leslie.

"Leslie?! Leslie?!" Kyle yells.

She runs to the phone, but as she is picking it up Bethany runs in.

"I already called 911," Bethany says, leaning over Leslie with a wet paper towel blotting it on her face in an attempt to wake her up.

Leslie mumbles something, and Kyle leans in closer to hear her, holding her hand, trying not to cry. The paramedics arrive and place Leslie on a gurney. Kyle grabs her purse and phone and follows them in the elevator. The Paramedics grab an IV bag and place an oxygen mask over Leslie's face. They begin to ask Kyle Leslie's name, date of birth, whether she knows if she's allergic to any medications.

"Her name is Leslie McCall, her date of birth is March 6th 1988, I am not sure whether she is allergic to any medications. I have texted her husband he will meet us at the hospital and will be able to answer the rest of your questions," Kyle explains.

Kyle sits in the waiting room, and the doctor lets her know that Leslie asks for her to be in the room with her. The doctor walks into the room with Kyle and explains what happened.

"Ms. McCall, you are severely dehydrated, and you are about 6 weeks pregnant."

"I know, I just wasn't sure how far along I was," Leslie says.

"We have gotten you started on some IV fluids, but we would like to run a few more tests to ensure everything looks okay. You will have to go down to have an ultrasound shortly and I will be back to speak to you afterwards," the doctor says as he pulls the curtain open and walks out of the room.

Kyle pulls the curtain shut, and sits in a chair next to Leslie.

"How do you feel Les?" Kyle asks.

"Tired as hell. I was fine earlier this morning, but soon as I walked into your office I started feeling lightheaded and the next thing I remember was being in the ambulance. Did you call Mike?" Leslie asked.

"Of course. I texted him. I know he was in a meeting and was afraid he'd miss my call but I know he is always on his phone texting or emailing, so I know he will see the text far quicker that a voicemail," Kyle explains. "Les, you have to tell Mike. He called me earlier saying he thought you might be pregnant and I felt terrible knowing I've known you were pregnant and couldn't say anything." Before Leslie can respond, Mike pulls the room curtain open and walks in with tears in his eyes.

"So neither one of you were going to tell me?"

Kyle turns around and reached for Mike's hand. Mike pulls away from her.

"What, you were going to murder my baby Les? Is that what you were going to do?"

"No, Mike I…" Leslie starts.

"I do not want to hear anything you have to say right now."

"Wait, Mike. Calm down. It's not what you think at all," Kyle says.

"Are you kidding me right now Kyle? I sat on the phone with you this morning and–" he stopped in mid-sentence. "Since you two are so fucking close and want to lie and cover up for each other, maybe you should take up residence together as well. You are not welcome in my home," Mike tells Leslie with a look Leslie has never seen on her husband's face before. "I will have your stuff sent to you. And Kyle, I thought you were my sister. I thought you would never lie to me, but I guess bitches stick together right?! You can find someone else to represent you. Fuck you and your business!"

Mike walks out of the hospital room in a storm.

"Mike wait," Kyle says, but decides not to chase after him. I've never seen him this angry before. Why don't you stay over tonight give him time to cool off, and go home in the morning? Then the two of you can talk this out."

"Kyle, I wasn't' going to kill our baby. I swear I wasn't! I was going to tell him this weekend, I had it all planned out, Les confesses.

"Les, that's the problem. You didn't need a plan. You just needed to tell your husband. I hate to kick you when you are down, but if the basis for the majority of your fights was a baby, when you found out, you should have told him. He is heartbroken Les, and I am partly responsible for his heart breaking, Kyle admits.

Leslie begins to cry.

"Kyle, I am so sorry for putting you in the middle of this, I just didn't know who else to talk to. Kyle, he kicked me out of our house," she says crying.

"He's just upset. We both know he is very reactive. Let's give him the night, and give him a chance to calm down and think. There is no way he is really going to put his wife and mother of his child out. Now, he may never speak to me again, but you two will be okay."

Leslie begins to cry again.

"Les, I am not mad. I understand why you told me. I will talk to him. We have been friends a long time, and I am sure he will eventually come around. He needs time. All he's been talking about lately is wanting to have a baby, so he is hurt and feels betrayed, and I understand his side of things as well," Kyle explains.

"But let's talk about you. You have to take better care of yourself Les. You scared the shit out of me today. You're eating for two, which means eat for two lady!"

"I know, I have been eating. Today was just one of those days where I didn't have an appetite and what I did manage to eat I threw up! And I would have grabbed a Gatorade, but I just had to much going on at once."

"Well, you absolutely have to do better my love muffin," Kyle says kissing her on her forehead. "Don't worry, everything will be okay".

A man in scrubs pushing a wheelchair enters the room and pulls the curtain back. He greets the ladies and asks Leslie for her name and date of birth, double checking it against her arm band and his clipboard.

"Mrs. McCall, I'm here to take you down to Radiology for your ultrasound," the man says.

"Can she come with me?" Leslie asks the man, pointing towards Kyle.

"Of course," the man responds.

Kyle helps Leslie out of the bed and into the wheelchair.

Chapter 10

When Friends Fight....

"Hey girls, I'm sorry I'm late," Evian says taking a seat at the table.

"It's okay, we ordered you some wine," Leslie replies. "Okay ladies, I wanted us to sit and have dinner and catch up, but I also wanted us to talk about what we are going to do about Tan and Kyle."

"I don't know. I tried to get them together and invited them to dinner. Kyle walked in and then straight out as soon as she saw Tangi there," Evian says.

"Wait, are you kidding me?" Leslie asks.

"No, I am not kidding. She literally saw Tangi, rolled her eyes and walked right back out the door.

"Well, I proposed a private mediation and meditation, that I would help facilitate and Tangi was not here for it at all. She said she didn't need it, that Kyle is the problem and she refused to talk to her," Asia announces.

"This is ridiculous, those two have been friends for too long," Leslie says.

"That's true, but both me and Evian tried to warn Tan not to make such a short notice request, but she wouldn't listen. She just knew Kyle would say yes, Asia says sarcastically, "and if you ask me the middle ground, Kyle's offer was very fair, in my opinion."

"Okay, well I don't want to get entangled in taking sides, I just want to repair the damage the best way we can," Evian states.

"Hold on E. I am not taking sides, I am stating the facts, and the fact is that Tan was selfish for making that type of request so short of notice. And then, turning her nose up at Kyle's counteroffer was BS and you know it!" Asia protests. "I get that Tan is 'your girl' but this is about right and wrong, and Tan was dead wrong."

"Wait, A. I am not accusing you of taking sides, I'm just saying I just want to get them to make up so we can go back to a five-some in oppose to the foursome we have been forced to endure for the past month. I am so sick of having to choose who to invite between the two of them, its draining," Evian explains.

"Okay stop!"Leslie quietly yells. "I cannot deal with another fight between friends. Let's just focus on the task at hand, which is getting these two back together."

"Yes, you are right Les. E, I'm sorry, I love you and I don't want to fight," Asia says, grabbing Evian's hand.

"No, I'm sorry A. I am just so tired of feeling stuck in between their crap," Evian says, squeezing Asia's hand.

"Okay, I have an idea. Neither of them have plans tonight. Let's invite them to karaoke, you know neither will turn down an opportunity to act like Whitney Houston," Leslie says laughing. "Maybe once they start having fun they will let their guard down and be open and ready to just talk, or at minimum let it go."

"Do you think that will work? Evian asks.

"Only one way to find out, right? What's the worst that could happen?" Asia asks. "I'll text

Kyle, who's going to text Tan?" she asks immediately looking over at Evian.

"I'll text Tangi," Evian says, smizing back at Asia.

"Okay, let's eat. I 'm starving. I mean, you all are just starving me and my daughter-to-be," Leslie says.

"Wait, Les, you're having a girl?!" Asia yells, not realizing she has drawn attention to their table.

"I don't know yet, but I really want a daughter," Leslie says smiling.

"Awww Les! I am so excited to meet her," Evian says.

"That's right E, speak it into existence," Asia says, snapping her fingers in the air. Leslie breaks out in a laughing fit, "You are so dramatic for someone so centered," she says, looking at Asia.

"Duh! Hello, have we met? I am Asia, actress extraordinaire," Asia says dramatically, extending her hand towards them.

All the ladies laugh.

Still laughing Asia picks up her phone to text Kyle.

Asia: Hey muffin, wanna go to karaoke? I am feeling like letting my inner Beyoncé out, lol!

Kyle: LMAO! Okay, I'm feeling a little Chaka Khan. What time?

Asia: Is 8 okay?

Kyle: Sounds like a plan. I will be there with my vocals warmed up…LOL Let me get some tea with honey.

Asia: I cannot take you today. OK honeybee, see you soon!

Kyle: smiling face emoji

"Okay I did my part, E. It's on you now," Asia says, showing her phone to all the ladies.

"Okay, okay! I'll text Tan now," Evian says laughing.

Evian: Hey Tan, what are you up to?

Tangi: Nothing girl. Some sketching, nothing major. What's up?

Evian: Feel like meeting up for karaoke? Leslie thinks she is in the mood for singing LOL

Tangi: Sing what? A lullaby? LOL the baby is the only one who wants to hear her sing! LMAO

Evian LMAO So you're coming? And Leslie says you're a hater.

Tangi: Yes, I'll come, and she's right! I hate her singing LOL ! What time?

Evian: We should get there around 8

Tangi: Okay, see you then.

"Okay she's coming," Evian announces to the table. Now let's eat before this food gets cold."

"Too late, Leslie and I have already started eating," Asia says laughing.

"I should've known you already started eating greedy, and Leslie has an excuse," Evian says shaking her head smiling.

"What time did you tell Tan?" Asia asks.

"8:00, but we all know that means closer to 8:30 or 8:45," Evian replies.

"That's so true, she is always late for everything. I don't know how her clients deal with it," Leslie says.

****

Kyle pulls up to the karaoke lounge, and pulls her phone out of her purse to see a text from Patrick.

Patrick: Hey, I stopped by your office a coupled of days ago to see if you wanted to go to lunch, but Bethany said you were in meetings all day. Are you purposely avoiding me?

Kyle: Don't flatter yourself. As you well know, work comes before everything even lunch.

Patrick: What are you up to now?

Kyle: Out with the girls.

Patrick: Where?

Kyle rolls her eyes, puts the phone back in her purse and heads inside.

She walks in and sees Evian and Leslie on stage howling the lyrics to what sounds like a Diana Ross song. Scanning the room in attempt to see where the ladies are sitting and who else is there, her eyes stop at Asia sitting in a large booth in the back of the lounge, and beside her is Tangi, laughing without a care in the world.

Her first thought is to turn around and walk away, but instead she takes a deep breath and walks towards the booth, all smiles and thinking to herself, "Be nice Kyle."

"Hey A," Kyle says as she gives her a hug and kiss on the cheek.

"Hey girl!" Asia yells smiling.

"Hey Tan," Kyle says giving her a side hug before taking a seat next to Asia.

"Hey girl," Tan responds as she continues to write her song of choice on a small piece of paper. She folds it in two, gets up from the table and walks over to the DJ.

"So were you going to tell me Tan was going to be here or is this some sort of friend intervention setup?" Kyle asks.

"The latter, but please stay and have an open heart," Asia confesses holding Kyle's hand.

"I have no problem having a good time while clearing up this foolishness," Kyle responds smiling sarcastically. "So have you sung anything yet?"

"No, not yet. I have been trying to channel my inner diva," Asia says, closing her eyes and flipping her hand palms side up as if she was meditating.

"Girl, you are absolutely crazy," Kyle laughs.

"What is crazy over here doing? Praying for the universe to bless her voice?" Tan says as she walks over and takes a seat.

"That's what she should be doing," Kyle responds smiling.

"You two are going to be so jealous when I get up there and tear the house down," Asia says, writing her song down, folds the piece of paper in her hand, hiding it like it's a good poker suit.

"Yes, I feel the greatest of envy penetrating my soul as we speak," Kyle says winking and sticking her tongue out at Asia.

Evian and Leslie return to the table laughing.

"Hey Kyle!" Leslie says smiling from ear to ear.

"Kyle, girl you are late," Evian says hugging her tightly.

"Why hello ladies," Kyle replies.

"Next on the stage…Tangi!" the DJ announces over the microphone.

"I guess I am up next," Tangi says smiling and walking toward the stage. The ladies are laughing and discussing their next song picks when the music cues for Tangi.

"Wait, is she singing bad blood by Taylor swift?" Leslie asks, quickly realizing she maybe should have said that to herself.

"I'm sure it is not for Kyle," Evian says.

Kyle furiously writes her song down and walks it over to the DJ. Tangi continues to sing, pointing in the direction of Kyle as she walks back toward the booth.

Asia put her hand over her mouth, "I think this song is for Kyle guys," she says.

Kyle looks so calm, maybe she's taking the high road?" Leslie suggests as Kyle approaches the table and takes her seat.

"Kyle, you okay?" Evian asks.

"I'm fine, Kyle says smiling, listening and watching Tangi sing.

The waitress walks over to the table, "Can I get anyone anything?" she asks.

"Yes, can I have Belvedere and club soda? And can you make it a double with lime?" Kyle asks.

"Yes ma'am. Anyone else?" the waitress asks.

"No we're okay for now," Evian says, looking at Kyle with a puzzled look.

"What?" Kyle asks looking at Evian.

"A double? Are you sure you're okay?" Evian asks.

"Yes I am perfectly fine," Kyle responds smirking.

Tangi walks back over to the table.

"What do you want to drink Tan?" Kyle asks.

"Oh, I will take a Manhattan," Tan replies with a smug look on her face.

Kyle signals for the waitress, who walks right back over.

"Can I also order a Manhattan? And put it on my tab," Kyle says as she passes the waitress her black credit card.

"Okay, it's about to be a shit show. Kyle never uses that damn black card," Asia whispers to Leslie.

"Are you serious?" Leslie whispers back.

"Yes, she only uses it for work related expenses," Asia says.

"Should I make up a reason for her to bring me home?" Leslie asks.

"No, when she's like this, you just have to let her be," Asia says shaking her head.

"E and A, I will get you both some wine," Kyle announces. "Les, I will get you a club soda with lime, so you can look the part," she says winking at Leslie.

"Okay girl," the ladies say in unison. The waitress returns with Kyle and Tangi's drink orders.

"Can I also have a club soda with lime, and a bottle of chardonnay?" Kyle asks.

"Yes ma'am."

"Thank you so much love," Kyle responds. She takes a sip of her drink and smiles to herself.

"Next up is Kyle!" the DJ announces. Asia and Evian look at each other with anxiety in their eyes.

Kyle takes another sip of her drink. "That's my queue," Kyle says and walks to the stage.

The song begins.

"Okay, this is going to get ugly. She's rapping Cardi B's Bodak Yellow," Leslie whispers to Asia.

Tangi raises an eyebrow, picks up her paper and writes another song down, and walks it over to the DJ, nodding her head at Kyle. Smiling in acknowledgement of Tangi's head nod she continues the song. Tangi walks back over to the girls smiling, picks up her martini glass and takes a one long sip of her drink.

"Tan, you good, girl?" Asia asks.

"Hell no! I will show her what a Karaoke beef is," Tangi responds with an attitude.

"Tan, calm down. You two are acting like children. Why don't you both just talk?" Leslie pleads.

"Les, I'm good. I promise," Tangi replies.

Kyle walks back to the booth, grabs her cocktail, and takes a sip. Tangi walks away.

"Kyle, what are you doing?" Evian asks.

"Did you happen to ask Tan the same question? Or did you make your mind up that I was the one who was wrong? Kyle responds. "Once I saw that she was here I could have left, but I came in with an open mind and heart. I thought we could have fun and talk our issues out like adults. Clearly, she was not on the same page," Kyle explains. "Bad blood, really? and you have the audacity to ask me what I'm doing," she says, looking at Evian.

"Kyle I get it but–"

Kyle interrupts Evian before she can finish her sentence.

"Hold on! I do not want to miss her next song."

Kyle gets up and walks closer to the stage.

"Maybe this was a bad idea," Evian says.

"You think?! Petty Labelle and Peppermint Petty can't stop taking shots at each other. This is just a mess. I cannot take another minute of this, I have my own shit going on," Leslie says.

"What the hell is wrong with these two grown ass women? They're acting like they are fucking 12 years old! What's next, a cat fight in the parking lot?!" Evian asks.

"Well, in Kyle's defense, she came in ready to talk, but as soon as Tan sang her first song, all that went to hell in a hand basket," Asia explains. "At some point, you are going to have to stop jumping to Tan's defense and start holding her accountable for her actions," Asia says.

"Okay, I have had enough, I am going to ask Kyle to take me home," Leslie says. Leslie walks over to Kyle, who is standing on the side of the stage talking to the DJ.

"Kyle, do you think you can take me home? I feel lightheaded." Leslie asks.

"I know you just want to get me out of here, but yes, let me tab out and I'll take you home," Kyle says rolling her eyes. "I didn't even get to drink my second drink, what a waste."

 Walking to Kyle's car, Leslie asks, "What happens the next time you see Tan? Are you going to act like an adult?" Leslie asks.

"An adult yes, punk ass bitch, No! Clearly that is exactly what she thought she was dealing with tonight. She better be glad I'm over 30 and partially saved," Kyle says as she starts the car.

"You know how she can be. Why did you let it make you get so upset? You two should've talked and apologized to each other, and could have enjoyed the rest of the night."

"So because that's just the way she is, I'm supposed to let it go? No, not ever. I offered her a spot that I didn't really have and didn't have to offer and she basically gives me her ass to kiss. Not on my watch. Not adorning her with a dramatic soap opera slap prior to exiting is all I am sorry for," Kyle says.

Back at the karaoke bar, Tangi walks back over to the table.

"Damn Kyle left before my grand finale or before I could order another drink on her, since she wants to flaunt that stupid black card around."

"First of all, Tan, you're dead wrong. And second, you wish anyone would extend you some credit," Asia says.

"That's right, take up for your girl!" Tangi shouts.

"I am not taking up for anyone. I'm clearly stating the facts, right versus wrong, and you, my dear sweet girl, were wrong," Asia says, as she grabs her bag and walks away from the table and out the door.

"People call you selfish, impractical, and entitled, and I think you are doing a good job of proving everybody right," Evian tells Tangi. "I love you Tan, but this thing between you two needs to stop. Let's get out of here."

Chapter 11

When snakes are lurking.....

"Good morning," Evian says to her assistant, Todd.

"Good morning Evian. Jake would like to schedule a time to meet with you. He has called several times this morning," Todd replies.

"How is my schedule looking this week? Do I have 15 minutes to spare to speak with him?" Evian asks as she walks into her office and has a seat at her desk.

"Give me about 5 minutes to check," Todd responds, handing Evian a steaming cup of coffee.

She sips on her coffee and opens her laptop. Just as she is about to make a call, Todd walks in.

"You have 30 minutes free at around 2:00pm," he says.

"Okay, can you see if that time works for him?" Evian asks.

"No problem. I will get right on it."

Evian picks up her office phone and dials Phil's office.

"Hey Evian, what can I do you for?" Phil asks.

"Good morning Phil. I wanted to go over a couple of things with you regarding our expansion and also some other information that has recently been brought to my attention. I am booked all morning but I was going to have an early dinner at about 4. Would you be able to meet me at the restaurant so we can talk?" Evian asks.

"I think I can do that, just text me the info," Phil responds.

"Perfect! will do," Evian says. She hangs up and texts Phil the restaurant location and time.

"Todd, how many internal interviews do we have for the Entertainment Department expansion?" Evian asks.

"It looks like today you have a total of four," Todd responds.

"Okay, perfect. I have a draft version of the interview questions, can you please edit them to include space for me to write in my notes and print four copies please?" Evian asks as she hits the send button on her email. "Should be in your inbox now," she announces.

"Yes ma'am," Todd replies.

****

Interviewees go in and out of Evian's office all day, all four walking out smiling.

Todd knocks on Evian's door, and pokes his head in, "Are you busy?" he asks.

"No, come in. What's up?" Evian asks.

"How did the interviews go? Anyone looking at the leadership role?" Todd asks.

"They went pretty good actually. I think all will be able to either transfer or carry a load for both. No one for the leadership role yet," Evian responds. It is a lot to take on, because I will be asking for this person to do a good majority of the footwork for the expansion and continue to take care of their current client needs, if it's in an internal candidate. So I am sure this will be a longer road to identifying the perfect fit for this role," Evian explains.

"It sounds like a huge responsibility, but I am sure you will pick the perfect person to fit the job," Todd says.

Just as they start a new discussion about travel plans Evian needs Todd to make for her to go to Chicago to meet with some potential clients for the Entertainment Division, there's a knock at the door.

Jake pokes his head in, "I apologize, is this still a good time?" he asks.

"Yes, please come in. We were just wrapping things up," Evian responds as Todd walks out of her office. "Please have a seat," she says, gesturing to one of the chairs in front of her desk.

"Well, first, thank you for taking the time to meet with me, I am sure you have been very busy with interviews in addition to your regular workload," Jake says. "Second, I want to apologize. I know I have been a jerk, for lack of a better word, but I would like the opportunity to start off on a clean slate with you if that is possible. I am entering into my second month of probation and it has given me a moment to do some self- reflection. I have seen where I have fallen short and could have possibly done better, as well as taken a look at my attitude in relation to how I receive feedback from not just leadership, but also my peers," Jake explains.

"I am more than open to cleaning the slate and starting things off fresh, and I truly appreciate your apology. I hope you know that the decisions to put you on probation weren't some sort of punishment, we just wanted to bring the best out of you. I know you have the goods, I just want you to show us all you have them," Evian says.

"Would you be open to me interviewing with you for the new division leadership role in the near future?" Jake asks.

I don't see why not. Get with Todd and see when the next set of interviews are being conducted and have him schedule a time for you. But I want to be transparent, I am interviewing internally and externally for this role and I will be monitoring your workload and client relationships closely," Evian explains.

"I totally understand," Jake replies.

"Okay great, then I look forward to your upcoming interview," Evian says as she stands and extends her hand for a handshake.

"As do I," Jake responds shaking her hand and exiting her office.

Jake walks into the hall, nods his head at Todd and goes into his office. He picks up his cell phone.

Text to Todd:

Jake: Thanks bud, your advice worked. She agreed to allow me to officially interview for the Head of the Entertainment Division job.

Todd: No problem. Did you say everything I told you about self-reflecting and you being a jerk?

Jake: Yes! I said it all and she was eating it up. I won't forget you when I end up with not just the entertainment head job, but her job as well.

Todd: I look forward to you keeping your word. I am going out on a real limb for you.

Jake: Don't worry bud. It's all part of the plan. I got you covered.

Todd: FYI she's having a meeting with Phil at your friend's restaurant at 4pm today. Let the plan commence.

Jake: Perfect!! I will take care of the rest

Text to Bro:

Jake: She will be there at 4pm. You know what to do.

Bro: Are you sure about this? You are positive that this is how you want to handle this?

Jake: Dude! Please tell me you're not flaking out cause you've been dating her friend, who is a straight bitch!

Bro: No, I'm on your side, just checking that you're sure, cause when it starts we can't go back.

Jake: I'm good. Let's end this bitch.

Jake sends an email to Evian thanking her for her time and he looks forward to the opportunity to interview with her. As Evian is about to open the email from Jake there is a knock on the door.

"Are you busy?" Todd asks with his body half way in the office.

"No, just reading emails. Come in," Evian responds.

"So, how did your talk go with Jake?" Todd asks.

"It went quite well, actually. By the way, he should be reaching out to you to set up a day and time to interview with me," Evian announces.

"Okay, I will start looking at what you have available for your next rounds of interviews," Todd replies. "Well, I am glad that things sound like they are moving in a better direction. I know there was some tension between the two of you," Todd says.

"Honestly, I had no issue with him aside for some work related matters that we discussed, so I hope I was not giving off any negative or tense vibrations regarding Jake," Evian responds.

"No, nothing like that, the walls just talk around here."

"Well, be careful what rumors you subscribe to, just because they were spoken about doesn't make them factual," Evian says. "I have some stuff to finish up before I leave for the day. Have you had a chance to get my travel arrangements all situated?"

"Almost done, I just have to reserve your car rental," Todd says as he walks out of her office.

About twenty minutes pass before Todd pushes the intercom button, "You're travel plans are all arranged Evian," he says.

"Thank you so much. I'm getting ready to head out for the day. I'll have my phone if anyone needs me," Evian replies as she walks out of her office.

Todd picks up his cell phone and sends a text to Jake.

Todd: She just left for the day. And FYI no candidates for the leadership role yet.

Jake: Good

Jake: Don't forget what you need to do in the morning.

Todd: Don't worry, the flowers and bottle of wine will be gift wrapped and waiting on her desk before she gets in tomorrow morning.

Jake: Perfect.

****

Evian gets out the car, hands her keys to the valet, and walks into the restaurant.

"Hello, I have a reservation for two under Graham," Evian says to the hostess.

"Yes ma'am. Please come this way," the hostess responds walking her to her table.

"Thank you," Evian replies as the hostess lays the menus down on the table.   Leo walks up to Evian's table.

"Evian, hey! How are you?" he asks.

"I'm good Leo, nice to see you again. How are you? It's quite busy in here already," Evian responds.

"I'm good, and yes it's always busy, but that's a good thing," Leo replies.

"Leo, I had a question for you. Is there a way to schedule running reservations for about four to five people for the next three to four weeks? I have some work dinners I would like to have here if possible," Evian asks.

"Absolutely, you can give the dates to the hostess and she will booked them for you," Leo responds.

"Perfect, thank you so much. I was just sitting here thinking where I was planning to have the dinners and you saved me," Evian says.

"Not a problem, I should be thanking you. You could go anywhere, so choosing to have them here is an honor," Leo says.

Leo excuses himself and walks over to greet a couple more guests before walking back to the kitchen area. The waiter then comes over and takes Evian's drink order.

Phil walks into the restaurant, "I'm with the Graham party," he says to the hostess.

"Right this way sir," she says and walks him over to Evian's table.

"Hey Evian, sorry I'm a little late. I had to drop the boys off to soccer practice," Phil says as he takes a seat at the table.

"No problem. Will we need to make this quick so you can pick them up?" Evian asks.

"No, the misses will grab them. I am all yours," he laughs.

"Great, let's get your drink order in and then we can begin," Evian says. "Did you get my email? I had to send it via my personal email because Todd has access to my business emails and this information is highly confidential. And as much as I like him, he talks way too much," she explains.

"I did. That's very interesting. How did this information fall into your lap? Phil queries before placing his drink order with the waiter.

"Steele and Clark actually reached out to me once the news got around that I made partner. They said they were having a rough time keeping their business afloat and wanted to know if we may be interested in buying them out, which would come with all their current clients. I've already had several meetings with them to discuss how and what the buyout would look like. So, what do you think?" Evian asks.

"I heard that they were having some money problems, but I didn't know it had risen to the level where they were ready to basically unload their business. It sounds good. Let's get some additional details before we present this to Jack," Phil says.

"Not a problem. I am in the process of scheduling some meetings with them. Would you like to join in with me?" Evian asks.

"Yes, that would be great. Just reach out to my assistant so she can add them to my calendar," Phil responds.

"Will do. I think this will be a great opportunity for us and will add to our roster and reputation," Evian explains.

"I agree 100 percent," Phil replies.

Shortly after Evian and Phil leave, Jake walks in and has a seat at the bar. As the restaurant starts to empty out, Leo walks over and takes a seat at the bar next to Jake.

"It's about time you came out here, I'm on my third round," Jake says.

"You do know I am the executive chef here, and not a patron," Leo asks sarcastically.

"Calm down, don't get your panties all in a bunch, it was a joke dude," Jake replies. "Did she show up? Was she with Phil like I texted you? Was she a snobby stuck up bitch like she is at the office?" Jake drills off.

"Okay, you're starting to sound a little obsessed and stalker-ish," Leo replies.

"Stalker-ish? Where did you get that word from? That doesn't sound like you, that sounds like your girlfriend, and I am not obsessed. I am just sick of her walking around the office flaunting a partnership that should be mine," Jake responds.

"Can we please keep Kyle out of this? All I am saying it that for the last month and a half all you do is talk about how she dresses, speaks, wears her hair...Are you sure this isn't some sort of sexual tension you have for her?"

"Dude, she's hot as fuck, and I would definitely bang her. But do I want to date her?

196

Fuck that!" Jake says. "Did she show or not? he presses.

"Yeah, she showed. And the guy showed up as well."

"Did you take the pictures or not?"

"Yeah, I took them. I'll text them to you now," Leo says. *Man, this just doesn't feel right. What if Kyle finds out?* Leo thinks to himself as he sends the pictures from his cell to Jake's.

Jakes phone starts to vibrate on the bar counter.

"Thanks dude. These pictures are perfect! Want to hit the strip club?" Jake asks.

"No, I have too much to do here," Leo responds.

"Your loss bud," Jake says as he finishes his drink and walks out of the restaurant.

Chapter 12

Bad Company

Ding-Dong! Kyle runs to the door holding her gown up.

"Hey Leo, please come in. I am almost ready, I just need to put on my earrings and shoes," Kyle says.

"You're fine, take your time. I know I am a bit early, I figured we could grab a bite to eat before the gallery. Does that sound good? Leo asks.

Leo is dressed in a black tuxedo with every hair on his head is in perfect place, along with a low well-groomed beard.

"That sounds great. Wow! You look, um, very handsome," Kyle says. "I mean, I don't think I have ever seen you out of your running clothes. No! I mean I only ever see you in your running clothes, Kyle admits, feeling totally embarrassed. "Well, please make yourself comfortable. The bar is to your left, feel free to make yourself a drink. And if you

want water, I have a plethora in the fridge,"
Kyle says, quickly walking almost running
towards her bedroom.

"Thanks, can I get you anything?" Leo
asks, but Kyle has already disappeared.

Leo walks towards the bar, but then decides
maybe water would be best, and goes to the
fridge to grab a bottle of water.

"Your house is amazing," Leo says.

"Thank you," Kyle says as she walks out
in a long black and silver strapless gown,
complete with black strappy heels and
diamond jewelry accents.

"You look amazing," Leo says.

"Thank you, is that your favorite word?" Kyle
jokes.

"Huh? No, I...." Leo stutters.

"Relax chief. I'm kidding. Let me make you a
drink, you seem a little wound up," Kyle says
with a wink and a smile, motioning for him to
come into the living room.

"What can I make you, kind Sir?" Kyle asks from behind the bar.

"What are you having?" Leo asks.

"Me? Oh I'm going to stick with what I know and love. Kyle responds, holding up a beautiful bottle of bubbly and exclaims, "Champagne! Haha! What would you like? Wait, let me guess…Scotch? Kyle asks.

"How'd you guess?" Leo inquires.

"I don't know, you look like a Scotch kinda guy. Macallan 25 okay? Kyle asks.

"Yes, that's great."

"Straight or on the rocks?"

"On the rocks, please," Leo replies. "So, how long have you lived in Los Angeles?" Leo asks.

"Almost four years," Kyle says as she sips some champagne. "How about you?"

"I have lived here for about 10 years. I moved here from Paris," Leo says.

"Est-ce que tu parles français?" Kyle asks.

"Oh, you speak French!" Leo responds looking surprised.

"I speak Spanish, French, and Portuguese, thank you!" Kyle says laughing, lifting her glass in a toasting motion.

"Very nice. I speak French, German, and Italian," Leo responds, lifting his glass and lightly touching Kyle's.

"Oh, well excuse me," Kyle says, faking like she's clutching pearls on her neck.

They both break out into laughter.

"Okay, well I think we'd better head out," Leos says, finishing his drink and looking at his watch.

"Okay," Kyle replies, setting her champagne flute down and grabbing her purse.

Leo starts his car after they get in and Joe's 'I don't Wanna Be a Player' starts blasting through the speakers.

"Oh, I'm sorry," Leo says and he lowers the music volume.

"What station is that you we're listening to?" Kyle asks.

"Ha Ha, that's my Apple Music library playing. I know it's not Rihanna, but I like it," Leos says laughing.

"Oh I see you got jokes," Kyle says in a sarcastic tone.

"I mean, every time we run into each other on the trail I always hear Rihanna blasting from your headphones," Leo says.

"I'll have you know I listen to other stuff too" Kyle responds rolling her eyes.

"Okay, if we got into your car right now what would be playing?" Leo asks.

"Cardi B's 'Came Thru Dripping'," Kyle says.

"Cardi B?" Leos says laughing with a surprised look on his face.

"What's that face for?"

"I just cannot picture you cursing, let alone singing Cardi B. You are always so professional and reserved," Leo says.

"Don't judge me," Kyle says rolling her eyes again.

"No Judgement at all. I'm glad to know you aren't as reserved and conservative as I thought you were. Well, I guess we have to get back to our music appreciation conversation later," Leo says as he pulls up to a valet. "We're here."

Kyle reaches for the door handle, but is immediately stopped.

"Please do not touch that door handle," Leo says, as he gets out and walks around the car to open the door for her.

"Why thank you," Kyle tells Leo before leaving the car.

"Good evening Chef Castellanos," the Maitre D greets Leo as they walk into the restaurant. "Chef Roman has reserved a table for you and your guest in the wine room."

"Thank you," Leo replies.

They walk in to a room with four tables, low lighting, and countless shelves of wine bottles on all three of the glass walls from ceiling to floor. Leo pulls out Kyle's chair for her.

"Thank you. I don't think I have ever been to this restaurant before," Kyle says.

It's pretty new. It's only been open about a year and a half. The executive chef and I are longtime friends," Leo explains.

"It's a lovely place," Kyle responds.

The waiter comes over to their table.

"Chef Roman has planned a special menu for you and your guest. Have you had an opportunity to review our wine menu?" he asks as he pours water for both Kyle and Leo.

Leo points to Kyle to let her order first.

"Oh, I am sorry, I zoned out for a minute. Yes, can I have a glass of Chardonnay please? Kyle asks.

"And for you, sir? the waiter asks.

"I will have a Macallen and ginger ale," Leo responds.

"Very well, sir." I will be right back with those.

"So how many times have you been here?" Kyle asks.

"I have been here three times. I came for the opening, a special tasting the chef had, and then again for an early dinner," Leo says.

"Nice, I am excited to see what this special menu consists of," Kyle responds.

"So what are some of your favorite spots? Leo asks. Kyle catches herself zoning out again.

"Oh... there's way too many to name. I just love great food and wine," Kyle replies.

"You seem a little distracted. Is everything okay?" Leo asks.

"Yes, I am so sorry. I do not mean to be I just have so much on my mind. Sometimes I get caught up in my thoughts," Kyle says.

"Well, what's on your mind? Is it work?"

"No it's not work. I just got into it with a friend and it is really bugging me. I'm sorry, I will get it together," Kyle responds.

"What happened, if you don't mind my asking? Maybe talking about it and getting whatever is in your head out will help you feel a little lighter," Leo suggests.

"I am sure you have better things to do than listen to a story about two grown women going back and forth like teenagers," Kyle says.

"I don't mind. Maybe I can offer some advice that will help or at a least be a good soundboard for you," Leo says.

"Okay, well long story short version, one of my good friends asked if she could be featured in next month's issue. I originally agreed and told her what section she would be in and that I would set up a time for someone to come do a quick interview and take some photos. Little did I know, she wanted to be one of the cover stories, which is normally a several page article, so I felt insulted. First because it felt as if she was dismissing our process for how much work goes into an article like that. Not to mention, she didn't even meet the criteria we have to be featured in that section. When I confronted her about it, she said it wasn't that big of a deal and then mentioned how I featured a mutual friend of ours in the section she wants in the magazine. Mind you, I didn't pick that story, someone else did. I just approved it, and it met the criteria, which made it easy to approve. So basically it ended with me calling her entitled and selfish," Kyle says.

"Wow, I can see why you were upset. Did she offer an apology? Leo asked.

"Nope, not at all. I thought that maybe once she got home she would have thought about our argument and maybe called to apologize, but that hasn't happened," Kyle says.

"Well, I can only speak for myself, but when an apology is due, you have to give people time to sit in the silence of not having you around. I am sure she will eventually come around, especially if you two are close," Leo says.

"We are close, she's like family to me. And you are right, thank you, I feel lighter now." Kyle responds. "So changing the subject, tell me more about you. When did you know cooking was your passion?" Kyle asks.

"Honestly, I knew when I was really little. I was always in the kitchen with my mom, asking to help and bragging at dinner on what I helped with. Seeing people's response to food always made me so happy," Leo says smiling.

"That is really inspiring. So many people get stuck in what they think they should do, and not enough do what they love," Kyle says.

"I absolutely agree," Leo responds nodding his head.

The waiter rolls a large metal cart with several covered dishes on it towards the table.

"Oh wow! Is this all for us?" Kyle asks.

The waiter begins uncovering each dish, naming them one by one, and placing them on the table. Kyle couldn't wait to try them all.

"I hope you have a healthy appetite," Leos says winking at Kyle.

"I absolutely do. And I am so ready to enjoy this wonderful meal," Kyle responds smiling.

During dinner, the two enjoyed their conversation over various topics and ate every last bite of each dish. Kyle appreciated this surprise distraction from all of her current worries.

"The meal was to die for! I will have to add that restaurant to my go to list," Kyle says as Leo drives over to the art gallery.

"Yes, I love that place. I do not get to indulge there as often as I would like due to my work schedule, but it is one of my favorites," Leo says as they pull up to the gallery's valet area.

As they exit the car and begin walking towards the venue entrance, they notice photographers taking pictures of guests as they arrive onto the red carpet.

"You can walk a couple of steps ahead of me onto the carpet, I do not want you forced into a relationship via the paparazzi," Leo says.

"Are you sure? I do not want you to look like an odd man out. And I am your guest," Kyle asks.

"I am positive. Go ahead and do your thing. I will walk right past you and wait for you inside," Leo assures her.

Kyle let a very low soft breath of relief out. She was just thinking, Damn, how am I going to maneuver this?

Kyle walks towards the red carpet. The cameras are flashing and she stops on the red carpet to greet some of the photographers and columnists she knows. She also sees a photographer from her staff and winks at him as a sign of a good job for being here at the event. It may make a good article for the next issue.

As Kyle is posing for pictures, Leo walks past the red carpet into the venue, greets some of the guests and walks towards the bar.

"May I have a glass of champagne and a bottle of water?" he asks the bartender.

As the bartender hands him the drinks Kyle walks up. Leo hands her the glass of champagne.

"Why thank you kind Sir. Are you sticking to water the rest of the night? Kyle asks.

"No, but I want to be mindful. I am the driver," Leo responds.

"Okay then driver, let's take a look around," Kyle jokes, nudging his elbow with hers.

They walk around the venue talking and laughing.

"The detail on some of these masks is just phenomenal," Kyle says pointing to the gold and black Egyptian masks protruding out of the walls.

"It really is amazing," Leo agrees. "I will be right back. I'm going to go say hello to the artist," Leo says to Kyle.

"Okay," Kyle replies and she walks over towards the sculptures.

As she stares at one of the intricate vases in admiration, she hears a familiar male voice.

"This is one of my favorites."

She turns and sees Patrick standing behind her. Gathering herself to not seem flustered by his presence, she gives a partial smile.

"Yes, it is quite an amazing piece."

Kyle hadn't seen or spoken to Patrick in almost two years.

"You look stunning Kyle," Patrick says gazing deep into Kyle's eyes.

"Thank you," Kyle responds stepping to the side creating some space between the two of them.

"How have you been?" Patrick asks, continuing to hold his gaze at Kyle.

"You know, the same ole same. Busy as hell.

"How is everything with you?" Kyle asks, wishing she could end this conversation, but not wanting to appear rude.

"I have been really good," Patrick responds.

Damn he still looks good, and he's wearing that cologne. Ugh! Kyle thinks to herself.

"I am so glad to hear that."

"Well, I'm going to go grab a glass of champagne –" Kyle starts.

"Here you go," he hands her a glass of champagne before she is able to finish her sentence.

"You know I am not a champagne drinker, but I didn't want to be rude to the waitress that handed me the glass," Patrick says smiling at Kyle.

"Thank you," Kyle says, taking the glass from his hand. She notices that the KP tattoo in between his thumb and index finger is still there. Kyle had hers covered up shortly after their break up.

"Kyle, can we do lunch?" Patrick asks.

Her heart starts to race. Trying not to appear anxious or nervous, Kyle keeps her composure and smiles.

Umm…I am not too sure. My schedule is crazy right now," Kyle replies.

"Well, I will call or text you and we can plan something when you are free," Patrick says.

"Okay, well it was really nice bumping into you. Enjoy the rest of your evening," Kyle says, as she lightly taps his arm. Before Patrick has the opportunity to continue the conversation with her, Kyle walks away and disappears into the crowd.

Taking a big sip of her champagne, she attempts to erase away the memory of her brief run-in with Patrick. She finds Leo and walks to him.

"This was an amazing show," Kyle says.

"I know, I was just telling the artist how amazing his work was," Leo responds. "Have you gotten a chance to see everything?" Leo asks.

"I think I have. Have you? Kyle responds.

"Yeah, are you ready to go?

"Yes!" Kyle responds a little too excitedly and Leo senses it.

"Is everything okay?" Leo asks

"Yes, I am just a little tired. Maybe I had one glass too many," Kyle says, knowing she could have probably had 5 more before feeling woozy.

"Let me get you home so you can get some rest," Leo says.

"Thankfully tomorrow I am working from home," Kyle responds as she gets into Leo's car.

"Lucky you," Leo responds shutting the car door for her.

Kyle feels her phone buzzing in her purse.

"Do you have an early morning tomorrow?" Kyle asks.

"No not at all. I usually get to the restaurant around 11 or so, unless I have errands to run. Then I may get an early start," Leo replies. "Will you be out on the trail? Leo asks.

"Of course. I try not to miss a day if I can help it," Kyle responds.

"Okay, why don't we meet there so we can run together and then after have breakfast somewhere? Leo asks.

"Are you opposed to having breakfast at my place? I just want to be home and close to my laptop to get some last-minute things done for work while we eat. Is that okay?

"Sounds like a plan to me. What time would you like to meet up on the trail?" Leo asks.

"The normal time is fine, 7am," Kyle responds.

"Perfect," Leo repeats as they pull up to the front of Kyle's house.

"I had such a good time, you totally got my mind off all the foolery that has been going on lately. Thank you," Kyle says, lightly grabbing Leo's hand.

"No, thank you for your company," Leo responds as he gets out to open her car door.

"Tomorrow?" Kyle asks.

"See you on the trail", Leo responds.

"Goodnight. See you tomorrow," Kyle says giving him a kiss on his cheek and walks into her house. As Kyle walks into the house, she pulls her phone out of her purse and sees 2 missed calls and a text from Patrick.

"What the hell does he want?" Kyle says as she puts the phone on the kitchen counter and walks into her bedroom.

Chapter 13

We fall down…

"Hey Les, I'm so sorry I'm late," Tangi says as she takes a seat at the table.

"I ordered without you. You may deprive me of food, but you won't be starving my baby," Leslie says rubbing her belly with one hand and stuffing her face with a sandwich with the other.

"Look at that baby bump! Oh my God, I can tell your preggers!" How are you feeling? How's the baby? Do you know whether it's a boy of girl yet? Tangi asks.

"Good, good, and I don't know yet", Leslie replies laughing.

"How are you and Mike? Have you two spoken?"

"No, I have called and called, but he won't return my calls," Leslie responds.

'Are you kidding me? It's been over a month, he needs to cut the crap!" Tangi says.

"He has every right to be upset, I just wish he would talk to me and let me explain. But I know you didn't come here to talk about my issues, what's up?" Leslie says.

"I need your legal advice. My investor/silent partner sent me an email stating that he will not be investing in my clothing line any longer," Tangi explains.

"Did you have a contract drafted as I advised you to do?" Leslie asks.

"No, I didn't really think I needed one. I mean, he and I were friends," Tangi replies.

"So you basically ignored my legal advice and now he is out," Leslie asks.

"Yes, is there anything I can do? Can't I sue him?" Tangi asks.

"Sue him for what? Breaching a non-existent contract? No, there is nothing you can do. Long story short, you will need to find a new investor." Leslie responds. "Why did he pull out? What happened?"

"He said he didn't feel like it was a safe investment anymore. And to add insult to injury, a couple of the clients I style have found new stylist due to creative differences, and when I told him the line would not be featured in FNBK next month, and may not ever, it made him nervous," Tangi says. "Things have gone from sugar to shit so quickly. The only thing that is keeping me level is the styling job I have on the morning show, and couple of new clients. Between you and me, Asia has taken over paying the majority of the bills, including the rent," Tangi admits.

"Have you tried getting a loan from the bank?" Leslie asks.

"I already did, but the amount won't cover all the overhead."

"Well, my dear, it is time to find a new investor. You know so many people in the industry, I am sure you can find one," Leslie says, attempting to cheer Tangi up.

"Yeah, I do. But the ones I have reached out to are listening to rumors about me being late for client appointments and not making my deadlines," Tangi says.

"Tan, are those really rumors. Come on, it's me. I know you," Leslie replies. "We talked about this earlier in the year when you were missing appointments with Mike and I to discuss and go over some of your questions. And I specifically said then, I hope this is not your norm, because if so it will not bode well for you."

"Okay! I have issues with time management, but my work should speak for me not some crazy time constraints that folks have," Tangi responds.

"Tan, are you serious? How would you react if you didn't get your fabric on time, or the makeup team came late for an event you were styling for?" Leslie asks.

"Girl, that's different. Those are vital to my being able to do what I do," Tangi replies.

"Tan, you may need to sit and re-evaluate your mindset, my love muffin," Leslie says.

"I think my mindset is fine, Les. What I need is some cash!" Tangi says. "Is there anyone else you can think of that may not be in the same circles of those who are talking about your "issues"?" Leslie asks making air quotes.

"I don't know. This has me all discombobulated," Tangi replies. "Can't you refer someone to me?"

"Unfortunately, the only person I do business with that works in or is even close being someone of interest is–"

Before Leslie can complete her sentence, Tangi interrupts her.

"Don't even say it, I do not want to hear her name. I do know someone who is sitting on a pretty large sum of money. Maybe I will be able to make this work after all," Tangi says.

"Can I offer you some just plain old friendly advice?" Leslie asks.

"Of course," Tangi responds. "You and Kyle really need to talk. I am not on anyone's side so I don't want to go back and forth on who is right and who is wrong. But I will say that stunt you pulled at karaoke was childish and totally uncalled for. Just so you know, I told Kyle she was childish for feeding into that," Leslie says.

"It was a joke! I'm not sure why everybody, including uptight Kyle, got so bent out of shape about it," Tangi says.

"Because it wasn't funny Tan and you know it. It was petty and it was spiteful. I stayed out of your original drama regarding the magazine because I didn't know all the information. But this I saw with my own eyes, and I didn't like what I saw," Leslie says.

"Well, for someone who isn't going to pass blame, that sure sounded like you blame me," Tangi says.

"Listen. I already said I wasn't going to go back and forth, because I knew you'd be all locked and loaded to plead your case. And quite honestly, Tan, I have a lot going on right now, so I'm in no mood for the back and forth," Leslie responds. You can take what I'm saying as me being your friend and wanting to see you do better, or you can be offended by it. It's your choice," Leslie says.

"You're pregnant and I don't want to make you upset. Let's just agree to disagree," Tangi says.

"Works for me," Leslie responds smiling. "Well, on that note, I have to get back to the office."

"Speaking of the office, how is that working out? With you and Mike, I mean," Tangi asks.

"Long story short, he moved into the condo we own downtown, only comes to the house to get clothes when I am not home, and he doesn't come into the office. He's been working from the home office during the day, again when he knows I'm not home, and schedules meetings at the client's office in order to not have to come in and use our conference room," Leslie says as her eyes begin to water up.

"Les, I—"

"I do not want to talk about this. I'm going to go. Since you are in financial disarray, I'll get lunch. Think about what I said. I love you Tan," Leslie says as she gives Tangi a hug and a kiss on the cheek before leaving.

Tangi picks up her phone and texts Leslie:

Tangi: Les, I swear I didn't mean to upset you. I am so very sorry. I love you and I am praying for you and Mike.

Leslie: I know you didn't mean to upset me, it's not your fault. I'm just an emotional mess right now.

Tangi opens her laptop to check her email to see if any of the people she's reached out to have sent a response about investing in her line. Every email she received reads: Ms. Childs we regretfully decline…

This is a nightmare, what am I going to do if I cannot get a new investor? Tangi says to herself. She motions for the waitress and orders a glass of chardonnay.

"I hope this is some money calling," Tangi says, hearing her phone vibrate in her bag.

"Hello?" Tangi says.

"Tangi, darling, it's Helena."

Tangi rolls her eyes remembering their last conversation. *She must need me back,* she thinks to herself.

"Hello Helena. How are you?" Tangi asks sounding as upbeat as possible.

"Darling, I heard you were having some issues with investors for your venture." Helena replies.

"Where did you hear that?" Tangi asks.

"Darling, this is a big but small city, word gets around. In any event, I think I may have an investor for you, however, they have asked to be anonymous and need to know exactly how much you need. Also, they have some provisions. They would like to see the business plan and also the timeline for your grand opening. And lastly, they have some concerns regarding your time management and asked has whatever was causing these issues been resolved?"

"I think the assumption is you may have been going through something and weren't focused."

Tangi removes the phone from her face and stares at it with her mouth open in shock. "What the...?" she whispers to herself.

"Hello, are you there?" Helena's voice comes through the phone.

"Yes, yes. I'm here," Tangi responds.

"So what do you think darling?" Helena asks.

"Let me get back to you Helena. I have some other investors who have recently reached out to me, so let me mull the offers over and make a decision," Tangi says.

"Okay, but this offer won't be around too long, so make haste my dear. I will let you go now. Kiss kiss," Helena says and disconnects the call.

"Is she off her rocker? And who the hell is this investor with all these provisions?" Tangi says to herself. "How dare they insinuate that I have some sort of problem! I will stick to plan B. I am not going to be treated like some sort of irresponsible teenager for some money," Tangi says to herself as she packs up her stuff, lays some cash on the table and leaves the restaurant.

****

Asia is in deep meditation in her room, and suddenly hears someone walk in through the apartment front door.

"A, you home?" Tangi calls out to her. Asia does not respond.

Tan hears the sound of the ocean and the smell of lavender coming from Asia's room. She knocks and walks right in.

"A, did you hear me calling you girl?" Tangi asks.

Asia continues sitting with her legs crossed and eyes shut. She does not answer, only putting her finger up to her lips to gesture Tangi to be quiet.

"Ugh!" Tangi sighs heavily as she rolls her eyes and walks out of Asia's room.

She walks into the kitchen, grabs a bottle of wine out of the refrigerator and a wine glass from the dishwasher, walks over and plops down on the sofa.

Asia walks out of her room a few minutes later.

"Well, if it isn't my exasperating roommate," Asia says as she walks into the living room. "What was so important that you made the conscious decision to attempt to interrupt my daily meditation? You know that if my door is closed and the ocean is going, please do not disturb. Considering you have a nice chilled glass of rosè in your hand, clearly you're not bleeding or dying," she says sarcastically.

"I'm not dying, but I am in financial peril," Tangi says.

"Okay, what's new?" That's been the case for the last two months. I still don't see the emergency," Asia responds.

"A, this is serious. I need your help," Tangi says.

"And you have my help, so what is today's crisis?"

"A, I need you to invest in my line," Tangi says as she takes a huge gulp of her wine.

"Tan, you know I cannot do that, hence why I thought I would do my part in helping you save more money by taking on paying the rent and all the bills for the apartment," Asia says.

"But A, you have the money, you sold your condo in Miami for like $1.5 million. I only need $200,000," Tangi says.

"Okay Tan, I'm going to act like you didn't just say that. No one, and I mean no one is privy to that money. That money is for me to invest in my own business should I decide to go that route. I have no interest in the fashion industry, whatsoever, so why would I invest in a clothing line? What, as a favor? A $200,000 favor? I'm not 50 Cent, and if you think he is bad when it comes to wanting his money back, girl, I will forget all my zen training and drag you through these streets. Fifty ain't got nothing on Crazy A," Asia says.

"Really Asia?! I can't believe that you are acting this way. I appreciate all you are doing, but to throw it in my face is just not cool. And then to imply that you wouldn't get your money back or some sort of return on your investment is insulting. It's as if you believe I am going to fail," Tangi responds.

"As usual, you are missing the point and being selfish. My reasoning has nothing to do with me thinking you will fail, number one. Number two, you have no right to expect that I would bail you out just because we are friends. And lastly, and most importantly, it's my money! My money to do whatever I choose to do with it. Hell, I may give it all away to charity, but that would be my right because it's mine! I can't even continue with this conversation," Asia says as she grabs her purse and keys from the kitchen counter and storms out the front door.

Asia paces up and down the hallway, "Calm down girl, calm down," she says to herself. She reaches in her purse and searches for her cell phone as she pushes the down button on the elevator. As it opens up, Evian is there.

"This must be divine intervention! I was just about to call you and ask could we meet and talk," Asia says.

"What's wrong? Why are you all red and flustered?" Evian asks.

"Tan has lost her mind. She has risen to a whole new level of selfishness. I can't talk like this, I need to calm down. Can we go somewhere and eat or maybe even have a drink?" Asia asks.

"Sure, let's go to the wine bar and kill two birds with one stone. They have food and wine," Evian says smiling in an attempt to make Asia laugh.

Asia takes a deep breath and lets out a huge sigh, "Okay, that works," she says.

"I'll drive so you can get your Zen back on our way there. I don't know what Tan did and I am scared to find out. I haven't seen you this upset in a long time," Evian says.

As Evian drives to the wine bar, she touches the screen of her radio and plays 7 Rings by Ariana Grande. Asia immediately starts bopping her head and smiles.

There's those dimples we love," Evian says.

"You know I love that song," Asia says laughing. Your friend asked me for $200,000," she says abruptly.

Evian pauses the music.

"Wait, she did what?"

"I know you heard me girl," Asia says as they pull up to the valet.

They walk in and take a seat at the bar.

"May we have the wine list and two menus please?" Evian asks the waiter. "Okay, let me get this straight. She asked you out of the blue for $200,000?"

"Yes, first she interrupted me while I was meditating, which definitely isn't the proper thing to do when you are going to ask someone for their money. Then, she went on about being in financial ruin and just blurted out she needs me to invest in her line. And when I said no, she had the audacity to say that I have it, so she couldn't understand why I wouldn't invest. And to top that off, she said I was acting like I do not believe in her," Asia vents.

"That is a lot of money to ask anyone to loan or invest. What is going on with her? I thought she had an investor and was just about to plan her launch party?" Evian asks.

"What's going on? Has she utterly lost her mind? I have supported her as much as I can, but this is just too much. I have plans for my money. Just because I haven't broadcasted it in the morning news doesn't mean I do not need it, nor have my own plans for it," Asia says. "See, this is when Kyle could help. She knows lots of money people, she literally is talking with new designers and investors all the time. She just told me that there's some confidential merger about to happen between two major designers. She couldn't say who, but she said it was huge, Evian explains."

"I wish those two would just make up already," Evian says.

"Evian, Karma has a way of catching up with us, and Tan has not been a great friend or professional. This may be her time to learn a very hard lesson about burning bridges. But I don't want to talk about this anymore. Let's order some food and wine and get a few giggles in while my energy is back in order."

Chapter 14

The Ultimatum…

Leslie walks into the house, and places her keys in the bowl on the counter. She makes herself a cup of tea and lies on the couch. Mike walks in the door fifteen minutes later.

"I got your text, is everything okay?" he asks. "Is the ba–"

Before he can finish, Leslie interrupts him.

"I am sick of this Mike. I tried to be understanding and give you some time and space to feel what you felt and process this, but enough is enough. I am over this. I get it, I messed up. I should have talked to you and not Kyle, it was wrong and careless. I know I hurt you. It was not my intention to keep it away from you. To be totally honest I was in shock and was confused," she confesses "I know that is not a valid excuse, but it is the truth. It has been 45 days since you moved into the condo. I kept saying every day to myself, 'he will be back he just needs time,' well times up buddy. It is time to shit or get off the pot. I am not going to allow you to drag this on any further. I'm having your baby, and additional stress is not making this pregnancy any easier. I haven't even told my parents about the baby, because I know the next word out of their mouths will be, 'When are you and Mike coming to visit?' My sister, Draya, took your side for about 2 weeks, and then asked when you were finally coming home. And when were we going to talk face to face not via email and texts. So let's talk this out. I have been asking for weeks, but you refuse to reply to my emails or texts that aren't work related. Neither one of us are leaving this house until we have some resolve to this one way or the other," Leslie firmly says.

"Leslie, you can't control me. You can't text me there's an emergency and then use the opportunity to make me talk to you. I was under the impression we were partners, we aren't. You only think of yourself. What you need, what you want, how things are going to affect you, and your feelings. And now because you are sick of me not being here you have the audacity to give me an ultimatum.

You gotta be kidding me. So now that you're hurt and upset, I need to make moves and decisions. Do you hear how that sounds, in all that talk you did? I have yet to hear the most important part - a fucking apology. Furthermore, how dare you drag your moms and pops into this! Really?! Do you really think that's supposed to make me pack up my stuff and come back home?"

He continues, "I am so glad you brought Draya in this discussion, because she and I spoke, and you know what she said? You owe me an apology, not excuses, just a plain old I fucked up, and I'm sorry. I told her if you would have or would just say those six words, I could let it all go and we could talk and all would be forgiven. You are not only my wife, you're my left and right hand. But of course, those words would never leave your mouth. While you were having your waiting to exhale moment, did you tell her that in the entire 45 days you have yet to apologize? I'm sure that part was conveniently left out. Well I didn't leave it out!"

Mike continues and asks, ""Are you sorry? Do you think you fucked up? Or was this just poor judgement on your part as you love to give that as an answer. Poor fucking judgement." Mike gets up from the couch and walks to the kitchen.

"How does what you did make you feel? Because I haven't heard that fall outta your ultimatum spitting mouth, either. And let's talk about your undue stress. You don't tell your husband that you are having his baby. The same husband who you knew has been wanting a baby and talking about having a baby with you for at least a year. I would say that your stress is self-induced."

"Do you know how badly I want to be the man who caters to his beautiful wife who is carrying their child?" Mike asks with emotion in his voice. "More than anything I want to see you every day, rub your feet and belly, cook for you. Les, I love the shit out of you. I left not just because of the shit you pulled with the baby, but because you come first for me in our marriage, I come maybe third to you in this marriage. I would rather let you go, than be your afterthought. You miss my birthday, anniversaries, and I don't trip. But the baby was the icing on a burnt cake. It is easy to talk yourself into thinking that I am been hypersensitive or taking this too far, because you weren't the one who was lied to and deceived. It's easy to make decisions about our life with no thought of how I feel about them. I guess men have no feelings, or is it I have no right to feel anything about your fucked up choices? I don't know if I want to be married to you anymore, that's why I haven't come back to the house, and I purposely make the distinction between this house, and not home."

Leslie felt that last point as intense as a bee sting. She winces at the pain of the words, like a knife piercing deeper and deeper.

"Even your partner in crime said you were wrong and should apologize. You know Kyle is like my sister, I take that back she is my sister. Kyle, A, and E are the only sisters I have ever had, the only family outside of my mom that I have. First you try to imply that there's something going on between us to deflect the baby conversation. Again, okay, I didn't trip.

But to put her in the middle of this whole pregnancy matter and not give a shit how that would impact our friendship is just another example of how selfish you are, Les," Mike states.

"Shit, Kyle has apologized a hundred times, but because I am so mad at the fact that my wife can't mutter an 'I'm sorry' I have yet to accept hers. Instead you hit me with the 'I get it. I messed up'. Who am I to you Les? I see the tears streaming down your face, and as much as I want to be the one to wipe them away and not cause them, this is your shit, not mine. Mike concludes. Without another word, he grabs his keys and walks out the door.

Leslie doesn't move. She stays seated on the couch, silently crying uncontrollably. Her phone begins to ring.

"Hello?" she says in a quivering voice, holding back more tears.

"Les, it's Kyle. Mike just texted me and said he thought I should come see you. Are you okay?"

"Leslie feels a lump in her throat, and tries to swallow to regain her composure, but can't. She starts crying out loud. "Leslie, what's wrong? I'm with Asia, we are on our way."

Leslie drops the phone and picks up a framed photo of her and Mike on their honeymoon in Barbados. She slides to the floor and wails as tears continue streaming down her face. "What they hell is wrong with me?" Leslie yells.

She hears a loud knock at the door. She gets up, unlocks the door and walks back to her place on the floor.

Asia runs into the house, "Les? Les?" She calls out.

As she walks toward the living room sofa she sees Leslie on the floor holding onto a framed picture sobbing.

"Oh Leslie!" Asia says as she sits next to her, passing her some tissues from her purse, and wraps her arms around her.

"What happened babe?" Asia asks. "Kyle is on her way in, she's on a work related call in the car."

"He's gone and he's not coming home," Leslie says as she wipes the tears from her face.

"What do you mean he's not coming home?" Asia asks. "What happened? All I know is while Kyle and I were about to head to grab something to eat, Mike texted her saying to check in on you."

Leslie begins to cry again.

"Okay, okay, just let it out," Asia says arms still wrap tightly around Leslie's shoulder.

Kyle walks in quietly almost tip toeing to the living room.

"Les, do you feel like talking?" Kyle asks as she scooches down to sit on the other side of Leslie. "Let me make you some tea and something to eat."

Leslie shakes her head no.

"Les, you have to eat. Little Leslie is hungry, I'm sure," Kyle says softly. "I will make something light and get you some tea and we'll sit here with you. You don't have to talk if you don't feel like it." "She gets up and walks towards the kitchen.

"Why don't you go ahead and get into some comfy clothes honey? You can't just sit here in your dress and pumps. Come on," Asia say as she gently pulls Leslie up from the floor.

"Okay," Leslie mutters out and walks into her bedroom and closes the door.

Asia walks into the kitchen.

"Did she tell you what happened at all?" Kyle asks

"All I was able to get out of her was he is not coming home," Asia replies.

"Do you think Mike asked her for a divorce?" Kyle asks with her hand on her chest.

"No, he wouldn't. He loves Leslie way too much," Asia replies.

"Well, he said something to make her think that he isn't coming back."

"What is he thinking upsetting her like this?" Asia asks.

"A, you know as well as I do he's hurt and super reactive when he's hurt. Hell, he's still not talking to me and I have apologized so many times. I even wrote a letter apologizing. None of that worked," Kyle says.

"Wait a minute! Back up, did you say that you wrote a letter? Like, typed or handwritten?" Asia asks.

"You always told me if you want people to know you're sincere, then all letters should be handwritten, so I wrote it by hand on my stationary paper you bought me for the opening of the LA office. But moving on to the matter at hand, she's hurting, he's hurting. What are we going to do? They're our family, A," Kyle says as she begins chopping up a bunch of lettuce.

"Do you think you can get Mike to agree to a meditation and mediation session with you and Les?"

"I think I can, but we have to get to the bottom of what happened," Asia says.

"Well, while she's in the shower can you slice up that French bread she has so I can make some crostini to go with this salad?" Kyle asks.

"Crostini? Now girl, I know you love to cook and can cook your tail off, but what is that chef teaching you?" Asia asks, smiling devilishly as she grabs the French bread out of its sleeve.

Kyle rolls her eyes and smiles big, "Whatever girl."

"Spill it lady," Asia says, pointing the knife playfully at Kyle.

"I haven't really wanted to talk about it, but he is amazing A. He cooks for me like almost every other night, and will either bring it to the office for me or have someone from the restaurant bring it to me. He is so freaking supportive and understanding, like he gets it. He gets me. He's not intimidated by my success and he can hold his own in a crowd.

"And the sex? I know you, Kyle. I know you have jumped on that poor man like an alley cat," Asia says silently laughing.

Kyle takes a deep breath, "Girl," she says as she exhales, "this man has met my body before, you hear me? He knows what to do, what to say, when to say it. The man puts me to sleep every fucking time," Kyle whispers.

"Bitch, stop!" Asia whispers back.

"Yes ma'am. Best thing since sliced bread – no pun intended," Kyle says.

"Kyle, I am so happy for you. You deserve to get some hair pulling, toe curling, knock your rigid ass out sex. And he's a good guy? Hallelujah! Thank you, Jesus! The universe has provided!" Asia says throwing her hands in the air and dancing in place.

"You play too much," Kyle says laughing. She has been in there too long. I'm going to go in there and check on her," Kyle says as she walks out of the kitchen.

Kyle walks to Leslie's bedroom and knocks on the door.

"Les?" she says as she walks in and hears the shower running. She walks into the bathroom and sees Leslie in the shower fully clothed sitting on the floor under the shower crying, listening to Jasmine Sullivan's Let it Burn.

"Asia!" Kyle yells to the kitchen.

Asia runs in the bathroom, sees what's going on and gets in the shower with Leslie, sitting on the floor of the shower next to her and wraps her arms around her. She motions for

Kyle to go. Kyle walks out of the bathroom and back into the kitchen.

"Leslie, babe, I know you're hurting, but you have to get out this shower and get dressed. At some point the water is going to get cold," Asia says.

Leslie pulls her head up from her hands, looks at Asia and smirks. She pulls her hair away from her face and gets up. Asia turns off the water and gets out the shower, grabs a handful of towels, passing a stack to Leslie.

"Look at me, I'm a mess! And look at you, your sweats and shirt are soaked! I'm sorry Asia."

"Sorry for what? Girl, please. I just need a robe till my clothes dry. I will throw them in your washer, no big deal."

"Where's Kyle?" Leslie asks.

"She's in the kitchen making you and the little one something to eat."

Leslie starts to dry off and slowly comes out of her wet clothes, walks over to her closet, takes and passes Asia a terrycloth robe and some slippers.

"Thank you," Asia responds. Leslie walks out of her room and into the kitchen. Kyle gives her a big hug.

"We are here for you babe," Kyle says softly.

"It smells good in here, what are you making?" Leslie asks.

"Well, I know you love tomato basil soup, so I made that with a small garden salad and some garlic parmesan crusted crostini," Kyle says.

"Okay, first I didn't even know I had the ingredients for that and second, what has that chef been putting on you?"

"Not you too, Oh my God. I cooked way before 'the chef'," Kyle says making air quotes.

"Yes, you absolutely could and can, but crostini?" Leslie asks smiling jokingly. Kyle makes a plate and bowl of soup for Leslie and pushes it in front of her.

"Thank you," Leslie says grabbing Kyle's hand.

"Mmmm, sure smell good in here girl," Asia says walking towards the kitchen taking a seat at the bar next to Leslie. Kyle makes a plate and bowl of soup and pushes it in front of Asia.

"Here you are my dear," Kyle says winking at Asia playfully.

"Thank you my love muffin," Asia responds.

The ladies eat in silence until Leslie states, "I think Mike wants a divorce."

"What makes you say that, Les? Mike adores you," Kyle says.

"I made a huge mistake. I texted him earlier and said it was an emergency and needed him to come to the house. When he got here, I told him I was sick of this. I was sick of him not being home and that basically he needed to make a decision. I told him I had not been able to tell my parents about the baby because of him, and that my sister agreed that him being gone this long was too much. I told him that his decision to not be home was causing me stress, which isn't good for me or the baby," Leslie says.

"What did he say to all that?" Asia asks.

"To say that it didn't go over well is a huge understatement. He was furious but calm, if that makes sense. I could tell he was beyond pissed, but he never once raised his voice. He said I was selfish for not telling him about the baby. He said that I have been selfish throughout our marriage and he hasn't made waves about it, but this was too much. He said I have said everything except I am sorry.

"Leslie, you did apologize, didn't you?" Asia asks.

"I told him I messed up. I should have talked to him and not Kyle. But no, I never said the words 'I'm sorry', if that's what you are asking," Leslie says.

"Les, Mike is our brother, and you are our sister. How can we help? We don't want to see you two in some bitter divorce. This can be fixed," Kyle says.

"I agree, this is fixable. But Leslie, you have to be willing to hear things like you heard today and apologize for them. I am more than happy to reach out to Mike and see if we can set up a real open and honest talk, and I will be there to mediate and make sure it doesn't go left," Asia says.

"What if he says no? What if he really does not plan on ever coming home? What if–"

"Stop it, Leslie," Kyle says, cutting her off. Mike loves you and you love him, I do not know how, but somehow the both of you forgot how to communicate with each other. I think A can help you get that back on track. But I agree you have to do more than take ownership for your flaws and faults you have to apologize for them. What good is knowing you messed up if you don't apologize for it?" Kyle says.

"We will do everything we can to help you two. We love you both," Asia says.

"You all don't know how much I appreciate you both. And you are right, if you can get him to talk to me, I'm in," Leslie says.

Chapter 15

Business, nothing Personal......

Evian walks into her office and sees a huge bouquet of red and white roses on her desk. She searches through them but can't find a card. She walks out of her office to Todd's desk.

"This is the fifth bouquet in the last 4 weeks. Are you sure there was no card attached?"

"Honestly, I didn't look. I just took them and put them on your desk," Todd replies.

"This is really weird, maybe I should call the florist and see if they have any idea who is sending them," Evian says.

"Oh no, you are far too busy with the expansion to worry about that. I will call for you and see if I can come up with any leads on where or who the flowers are coming from," Todd says.

"Really? I would appreciate that. I am really busy, but I would like to know who is sending them," Evian says.

"Of course, no problem."

Evian grabs a huge stack of binders off her desk.

"I am going to run over to Phil's office if anyone is looking for me," she says to Todd as she walks out of her office.

****

"Hey Phil," Evian says as she walks into his office and lays all the binders down onto a round table.

"Good morning Evian," Phil responds. "What's with all the flowers being delivered? You have a new beau in your life, Phil asks.

"I honestly have no idea who they are from, and there's no cards attached."

"I guess you have some sort of secret admirer," Phil jokes. Maybe they're from Jake. Maybe he's buttering you up for that leadership role in the Entertainment Division."

"Who knows, we did have a good talk and I think maybe we have cleaned off the slate and can start fresh," Evian says. "Okay, let's get started. I've spoken to the contact over at Steele

& Clarke and they have accepted all of our terms and are ready to draw up a contract. I think today will be a good day to meet with Jack and go over the Steele & Clarke deal. I don't want to keep him in the dark too long," Evian says.

"I'm on board with that," Phil says.

"Great, I have a meeting with him this afternoon. I'll just ask for you to come in at the tail end and we can present the deal to him then."

"Sure, what time is your meeting? I'm scheduled for a chat with him as well," Phil says.

"I believe it's at 2:00 until 3:00pm," Evian responds.

"That works, my chat is due to start around 3," Phil says.

"Okay perfect. I will leave all this with you to review and then we can present the deal later this afternoon," Evian says as she gets up from the table.

She walks back into her office to find Jake at Todd's desk.

"Can I help you with something Jake?" Evian asks.

"No, I was just asking Todd when you may have some time on your calendar to go over some new clients I'm signing on," Jake replies.

"Oh. Um, today I know for sure I'm completely book, but I'm sure Todd can find a spot for tomorrow if that works for you," Evian says.

"Yes, tomorrow is fine. Thank you," Jake says as he walks out of the suite and back down the hall.

"Todd, see if I have something tomorrow morning please," Evian asks as she walks into her office.

"Of course. I think you have an opening around 10 or 11 tomorrow morning. I'll send Jake an invite and see if that time is good for him," Todd replies.

****

Jake sits at his desk and pulls his cellphone out of his pocket.

Jake: She has no idea that today is her last day, does she?

Todd: Not a clue.

Jake: I see a bonus coming your way real soon! She will wish she would have signed off on your bonus instead of putting it on a probationary period now.

Todd: She basically gave me the same lines that she gave you. That my performance needed some work, and that she wasn't saying no to the bonus, just not now.

Jake: Well, you'll get your bonus and then some, you have my word bud.

Todd: I'll be waiting for my first check!

Evian sees Todd texting from her office, and shakes her head. This is exactly why he is on probation now, she says to herself. She picks up her cell and notices that it's 1:55pm.

"Oh, I have to get out of here and go meet with Jack," she says to herself, grabbing some binders off her desk and her iPad.

"I'm going to go meet with Jack and then I'm leaving for the day," Evian says to Todd, walking down the hall. She arrives at Jack's assistant.

"Hey, Jessica. Is Jack free? We have a meeting at 2," Evian says.

"Let me check," Jessica says as she picks up the telephone, "Mr. Hoffman, Ms. Graham is here for you. Go right in, Ms. Graham," she replies a second later.

"Thank you Jessica, and I responded to your email."

"Thank you, ma'am. I received it. I have sent the place and time.

"Great," Evian says, and walks into Jack's office.

"Hello Jack."

"Evian, please have a seat," Jack says. Evian takes a seat and lays her binder on the floor next to her chair.

"Evian, somethings have been brought to my attention that are quite unsettling," Jack says. He pulls an envelope out of his desk and pushes it towards Evian. Evian's stomach starts to turn as she opens the envelope and sees photos of her and Jack at dinner, photos of her with Steele and Clarke's contact person, and several cards from flower bouquets.

"What is all of this?" Evian asks.

"That is exactly what I wanted to know," Jack responds.

"Well, clearly they are pictures, but I don't have any idea what they mean, and I have never seen those cards before."

"Evian, it's been brought to my attention that you and Phil may have some sort of inappropriate relationship and it also has been reported that you placed Jake on probation as a form of retaliation due to him not accepting an advance you made towards him."

"Wait, what?! I don't mean to cut you off, Jack, but this is absolutely ridiculous! Did Jake tell you this?! I would never and have never made an advance towards him. And me and Phil?! Is that a joke?! Phil and I have been meeting after work to discuss a potential merger, and the man in the other photos is Michael Clarke, from Steele & Clarke."

"Jake did not initially tell me anything, someone else came to speak with me privately to inform me of a discussion they had overheard, and I quote, 'Ms. Graham stated that little shit Jake thinks he can says no to me. He will be a mid-level agent forever as far as I am concerned," Jack replies reading from a piece of paper.

"Who made that report? It is totally false!" Evian states.

"I am not at liberty to say, but you meeting with a competitor and not discussing it with myself or Phil is questionable," Jack replies.

"Did anyone reach out to Steele and Clark and ask about our meetings?"

"At this stage, I am not sure we can take the risk of keeping you on board. I have asked Human Resources to draft a separation agreement," Jack says, pushing some papers towards Evian.

"I am not resigning," Evian says as she reads the agreement. "I have no idea what is going on here, but I will be speaking with my attorney and the press!"

"Evian, please calm down. I'm willing to negotiate and offer you a severance package if you leave quietly."

"Well, it better be one hell of a severance package Jack," Evian says as she grabs her binder and iPad off the floor.

"Evian, how about you take a couple of weeks off with pay, and I will have HR work on a new agreement as well as the severance?"

"Fine."

Evian storms out of the office. She walks into her office, grabs her laptop, cell phone, and purse, and walks out of the suite to the elevator.

Jack steps out of his office, "Jessica, can you please call Phil and ask him to come over to my office?"

"Yes sir," Jessica replies.

"I'm going to go out on a limb and say that it didn't go well," Phil says as he walks into Jack's office and takes a seat.

"We are definitely going to have to offer her a severance. She threatened to go to the press, and she has friends in the media world. We do not need any bad press if we are going to close this Steele & Clarke deal without her."

"You're sure about this Jack? We can't stand to lose this deal. Remember, we made Evian partner because of her revenue potential. Losing her is losing a huge chunk of our clients, most of our top money makers," Phil asks.

"Jake's parents are very good friends with Mike Clarke He assured me that the deal is as good as closed with or without Evian."

"Then let's get with HR and see if we can expedite the severance offer and separation agreement. Will there be a non-compete clause? If so, I guarantee she will not sign it."

"No, I don't think it's needed," Jack responds. "Let her go work wherever she wants."

"Okay, let's see if we can get it to her by close of business today," Phil says as he walks out of Jacks office.

Jake walks into the partner's suite and into Evian's office.

"I think I'll have maintenance move the desk and credenza on the other side of the room. What do you think Todd?" Jake asks.

"I think you'd better get out of there, Phil is on his way over here," Todd replies. "He just sent me an email to ask you to come by his office, then said never mind he would go to you."

Jake walks out the office and heads out of the partner's suite, when Phil stops him.

"Jake, I was just coming to chat with you," Phil says. "Come over to my office for a minute."

"Sure," Jake says.

"Have a seat," Phil says as they walk into his office. "As you may or may not know, Evian will be leaving us. I just met with Jack and he tells me that you're pretty sure that you can close the Steel & Clarke deal."

"My parents and Mike are very close friends, he's like family," Jake says.

"Well, Jake, I want to be extremely clear about this. If you do not close the deal, not only will you not be referred for partner, but you will be fired. We a taking a huge risk on you and I, unlike Jack am not a gambling man."

"You have nothing to worry about Phil. I will have a signed contract for you in 45 days tops," Jakes says.

"Okay, that's exactly what I need to hear," Phil says.

Jake walks out of the partner's suite, into his office and pulls his cell phone out of his pocket.

Jake: Dude, the bitch is out!

Bro: They fired her?

Jake: Not sure, but I do know she's gone, and that partnership is mine.

Bro: I still don't know about this bro. You are ruining her career.

Jake: Don't get all soft on me now. She claims she's the best, so I'm sure she will land on her feet. I get your screwing her friend, but man up!

Bro: I keep telling you, leave Kyle out of this. I am not going to say it again!!

Jake: Okay, okay. Chill out bud. I'll be over your place later for my celebration shots.

****

Evian sits at a red light, quickly searching through her purse for her cell phone.

Group text: I was just asked to fucking resign or be fired!!! Long story, too much to text. Let's meet later for dinner and I'll tell you what happened.

Kyle: Are you serious??? WTF!!!

Asia: Where and what time???

Leslie: Did they give you something in writing?

Tangi: What kind of shit is that???

Evian: Let's meet at the Italian spot around 6.

Evian puts her phone back in her purse and pulls up to valet.

"Good afternoon, ma'am. Will you be joining us for dinner?"

"Yes, but more like a late lunch," Evian says smiling as she walks into the restaurant.

"Good afternoon," the hostess says.

"Hello, I am meeting with the Stein party for two I believe," Evian says.

"Yes ma'am. Right this way," the hostess responds.

"Jessica, I'm so sorry I'm running a bit late, I had some calls to make," Evian says as she takes a seat at the table.

"It's quite alright, Ms. Graham," Jessica says.

"Please call me Evian."

"Okay, Evian. I have wanted to talk with you in private about what happened today. I have some important information regarding the details of the conversation you had with Mr. Hunter this afternoon. Last week, I was asked to sit in on the meeting between Jake, Todd, and Mr. Hunter to take notes. I was told that it was highly confidential and nothing that was discussed was to leave the room. I know that I could lose my job by sharing this information with you, but what Jake is trying to do is wrong," Jessica begins. "Jake told Jack that he believes you were having an inappropriate relationship with Phil, had pictures of you and

Phil having dinner, sometimes drinks, very late at night at a private table in the back of some restaurant. He told him that he feels that he was being retaliated against for not wanting to date you. Jack asked why he had not come forward sooner with that information and Jake told him he wasn't sure until Todd confirmed his beliefs."

"Wait, I'm sorry, my assistant Todd?" Evian asked.

"Yes ma'am," Jessica confirms. "Todd proceeds to tell Mr. Hunter that he had overheard you talking about how good-looking Jake was and how you were going to ask him out, and about a week later he heard you on the phone saying he turned you down, and that basically you weren't going to promote him. Jake told them you had invited him for drinks several times, but he declined and didn't think much of it, until Todd told him what he overheard. Jake then went on to say he believed you were working on the side with Steele and Clarke, and had pictures to prove that as well. And for the record, Jack never spoke to Phil officially. He told him about the rumor and Phil denied it, and it was over. No suspension, no further discussion."

"I cannot believe this. This is a nightmare," Evian says.

"I probably should have said something sooner, but to be honest, I didn't think Jack would believe any of it. But when I saw his reaction during the meeting with Jake, I knew I had to speak with you. And he convinced Phil that they would just take over the merger with Steele and Clarke, stating that they would reach out to them after the investigation and you were asked to resign or be terminated."

"And Phil agreed?"

"Yes ma'am."

"When did Jack speak with Phil?"

"Last Friday afternoon."

"So right after I told him the deal was almost done and we would go over the paperwork this week."

"Don't you worry about your job. I give you my word this conversation will not be repeated nor mentioned."

"I truly appreciate your bravery. I know this could not have been an easy decision for you. You have been with Jack since the beginning."

It was not a hard decision Ms. Graham. I am a loyal employee, but I also believe in right and wrong, and this is wrong. I have seen how hard you have worked and felt it wasn't right that the boy's club mentality was threatening your career," Jessica says. "You should be expecting an email by close of business today with the new agreement terms, because they want to cut off your access to company emails."

"Jessica, I cannot thank you enough. I will be in touch, and I promise this conversation will not leave this restaurant."

Chapter 16

Confessions...

The doorbell rings. Kyle walks into the foyer.

"It's open!" Kyle yells, and then briskly walks back into her bedroom. "I am almost dressed, make yourself a drink," she yells from her bedroom. She walks into her closet rummaging through her racks of dresses.

"Dammit, I have no idea what to wear!" Kyle says to herself.

"Anything you wear looks good on you," a voice says from the closet doorway. Kyle quickly turns around startled.

"Patrick! What...? How...? What are you doing here?" Kyle asks.

"You haven't been returning my calls or emails. I really need to talk to you Kyle," Patrick responds.

"What do you want today? Make it quick, I have plans," Kyle says grabbing a silk robe and putting it on.

"Kyle, I was a jerk. I was scared and I didn't know how to tell you."

"Patrick, it's been two years since I last heard from you. Two years. So what now that you've gotten whatever out of your system you want me back?" Kyle asks.

"I didn't have to get anything out of my system. I just knew if I was going to come back to you I couldn't come half ass," Patrick replies, sticking his hand in his jacket pocket and kneeling down one knee.

"Kyle–"

"No, no, no!" Kyle says cutting him off. You cannot do this. You cannot just show up at my door, and drop a proposal on my doorstep. I am seeing someone and I..."

"Kyle, I didn't come here to upset you," Patrick says cutting her off. "Listen, I know I dropped in unannounced and that was wrong, but if you will please just agree to sit and talk with me. Give me a chance to explain, and if you still want me to leave you alone, I will. You don't have to answer now. I'll call you later and you can let me know your answer, but please think about it. Don't just jump off the handle as you normally do out of anger and say no," Patrick says as he places the ring box in her hand and walks out of the bedroom. As he's walking out he sees Leo standing by the bar. He walks right past him and out the front door.

"Let me lock my damn door," Kyle says loudly as she walks out of her bedroom. "Leo, I was just about to text you," she says wondering how long he had been there and how much he may have heard.

"Hey, I just got here. Was that someone from work?"

"No, it wasn't. It was someone I used to date. I really don't want to get to deep into it, just know he is in the past," Kyle says.

"You never talk about your past relationships, it's like that part of you is closed or off limits."

"It's not that it's off limits, I just find no reason to talk about the past, but in this case I understand why it may be important. He and I were together on and off for about 3 years. We had a lot of issues, but the main thing was he just didn't understand me, he didn't understand my work, my passion for what I do. He tried and I think he wanted to get it, but couldn't handle feeling like he was in a fish bowl. And I understand that. He saw me as a public figure, I didn't. I mean, no-one stops me for my autograph, but models and photographers will stop and ask to meet with me or someone from my team, wanting me to look at their headshots, their photographs, or refer a designer for me to check out. I have worked hard to make a name for myself, and I didn't want to keep apologizing for my success to him. I always felt like I had to fade my light a little so that he was comfortable. At the end of the day, he just felt like it was too much for him and didn't want to do it anymore," Kyle explains.

"I know you said on and off, is this an attempt at getting back on for lack of a better word? How do you know that you won't have a change of heart?" Leo asks.

"I know because I just do not feel the same way I used to anymore. I do not want to not be me to be with someone. Leo, I do not know where this is going to go with you and I, but I am in it 100%. You understand me, you get me, we have so much in common, and I believe I get you as well. You do not make me feel guilty about not being able to see you due to work," Kyle smiles. "Instead, you send me food and a bottle of wine. That may seem small or insignificant in your book, but to me it means a lot. Do not let a ghost from my past get under your skin," she assures.

"I'm not afraid of old ghosts, but I am afraid of what I have to confess to you," Leo says.

Kyle's eyes get big, "What is it?" she asks.

"A friend of mine asked me to do him a favor a couple of months ago. He told me that this woman had stolen a job from him and he needed my help proving that she wasn't what the partners thought she was."

"Please don't tell me this friend's name is Jake," Kyle says.

"Yea, it's Jake. He told me that Evian was making shady deals and that she didn't deserve to be made partner. That he had proof, but needed my help. So, I am the one who took the photos of Evian in my restaurant. He told me that she was doing business on the side with a competitor and that they would be meeting for a business dinner at the restaurant. All he needed me to do was take pictures, and that is why I took those photos," he confesses.

"I just recently learned the truth of what he really said and did with them. I couldn't talk him out of it. I tried a few times, saying to let it go, to understand that maybe her meetings aren't as shady as he thought, but he told me I had no idea the type of person she really was. But the more interactions I had with her at the restaurant the more I started to doubt his description of her. I had no idea he was going to go so far. He has some sort of weird obsession with Evian. I thought maybe he was attracted to her, but it's more than that. He is jealous as hell of her, and I just figured that out."

Kyle takes a deep breath.

"I thought you were going to say you had a wife or a girlfriend or maybe you wanted us to stop seeing each other. Any of those things I think I could have taken way better than this.

To find out that you are just a scumbag who uses people and helps destroy lives?! What the fuck?! Did you think that this confession was going to bode well for you? Did you think I would have a forgiving heart because you came clean when you could have just kept quiet and I would have never been the wiser? Wrong!

Do you know how fucking hard she has worked to be where she is? She had to start as a personal assistant with a whole Master's degree! Why you ask? Because she is a woman and men like you and your little buddy said they didn't think she had the 'stomach', when what they really meant was balls for sports management. They felt like she would never be able to earn the trust of male athletes. Do you know how many days she was at home crying because she didn't think she would be able to ever get her foot in the door? When they finally did let her in the door, they restricted her to female clients only! She worked her fucking ass off and is one of the most successful agents, male or female, if not the most successful! Just for you and your piece of shit 'friend' to take it away from her.

Who the fuck do you think you are? Better yet, what do I look like? You used me to get close to my friend and think a confession makes things okay?"

"Kyle, I didn't use you. I didn't even know she was a friend of yours until the day at your house when I dropped off the invite. And you're wrong, I definitely did not think my telling you was going to somehow sit well with you," Leo says.

"There is absolutely nothing you could say to make me want to hear anything else you have to say. I am done, please leave. Do not call, text, email, hell don't even send a smoke signal for me! The same way you let yourself in, see yourself out!"

Leo gets up from the couch and walks out the door.

Kyle walks into her room and sees the ring box lying on the bed. She sits on the bed and opens the box.

"Do not put it on your finger, girl. This is too fucking much for one day," she says to herself.

She gets her phone and takes a picture of the ring and sends it in a group text.

Asia: That's The Belle by Harry Winston.

Leslie: Leo proposed????

Kyle: No. Patrick.

Asia: Did Patrick hit the lotto??? Bitch that's a 6 carat yellow diamond!

Leslie: He didn't hit the lotto, but he did sign a huge deal. He bought that IT company that he used to work for. Our firm helped negotiate the contract and purchase. And before you all have a fit, it wasn't me or Mike, it was one of the associates who handled that deal.

Asia: Wait, how long have you two been back on speaking terms?

Kyle: We aren't, he had been calling and texting me, but I never responded. He just showed up at my door unannounced.

Asia: I know this is a bad time to bring up Tan, but she always gives good advice, even if she is a raving lunatic sometimes.

Tangi: I am sure that you sent this message to me accidentally, but my 25 cents is say no, he left you high and dry and never even did a check in or apologize for the way things ended, nothing. I vote no. Okay, I'm going back to my minding my business. T.

Leslie: Kyle, I have to agree with Tan on this one.

Asia: I am still in shock.

Kyle: I will talk to you all tomorrow, I'm mentally drained. Oh, and FYI, you won't believe who was involved in that ordeal with Evian and her job. Leo! You all's favorite guy. I'll explain tomorrow.

Kyle: @Tan <3

Kyle scrolls through her phone and stops on Patrick's name. She looks down at the ring again. Just as she is about to press the call button, she hears the doorbell ring.

"Who is it now?" Kyle says to herself, as she walks out of her room and to the door. She opens the door and sees a bouquet of peonies. She brings them in and reads the card.

'I know you are mad at me and may never speak to me again, but Kyle do not marry him. You said it best, he doesn't get you.' –Leo

"He heard that whole conversation. Good! Asshole!" Kyle says to herself and throws the entire vase of flowers in the trash can. She walks back into her room and picks up the phone and calls Patrick.

"Thank God, his voicemail," Kyle says.

"Hey, it's me. When you get this message call me, better yet just come through so we can talk. Okay, talk to you later," she says and hangs up.

Chapter 17

The Mediation...

Mike pulls into the garage of his condo when his phone begins to ring. Mike pushes the accept call button on the steering wheel.

"Hey Asia, what's up?"

"Hey, I need about an hour and a half of your time, can I come over?"

"Sure, you have the address?"

"No, text it to me, I'll be over in a few.

"Okay, I'll text you the address now."
Mike gets out of his car and gets in the elevator going up to his condo.

"Dammit, I forgot to pick up my dry cleaning," he says to himself as he walks in the door.
He walks into the bedroom, grabs a Columbia University t-shirt and some basketball shorts out of the dresser drawer and walks to the bathroom to change.
Just as he is about to pick up the phone to make a call, his phone rings.

"Hello, Mr. McCall. You have a guest," a man's voice says over the phone.

"Yes, please let her up," Mike replies. As he walks out of the bedroom the elevator door opens and Asia walks in.

"I don't know if I like that the elevator opens straight into the apartment," Asia says.

"Why not? You can't get up here unless the concierge physically walks to the elevator with you and scans his card for the penthouse," Mike says.

"I guess, it just seems unsafe," Asia replies.

"So, what's up?" Mike asks.

"Aren't you going to offer me some wine, juice, water? I mean anything will do. I am a first-time guest here," Asia says.

"Yes you are, and a pain in the ass already," Mike replies, walking to the kitchen. "What would you like princess? Mike asks sarcastically.

"What are you drinking? Asia asks.

"Probably scotch," he replies.
"Too strong for me, I will just have a glass of Merlot if you have it," Asia replies.

"Coming right up madam."
Mike opens a bottle of wine and pours a glass for Asia and himself. He hands a glass to Asia.

"Oh, I see you changed your mind," Asia says as she takes her glass and has a seat on the sofa.

"Indeed, I have. Now that you have your wine, what can I do for you?" Mike asks.

"Well, I want you to review this contract for me and tell me what you think and whether the terms seem fair. And if it needs revision, will you please do it? I will pay you for your time. I understand this is business," Asia replies, as she removes an envelope from her purse and hands it to Mike.

"A, are you really thinking about a moving?" Mike asks as he reads through the papers.

"Have you finished reviewing the contract? If not, I'd save all comments and questions until then," Asia responds as she takes a huge gulp of her wine.
Mike continues to read the contract, flipping the pages and tapping his chin with is finger.

"A, this is not just fair, this is a great deal. The terms benefit in your favor heavily. If this is what you want to do, I would strongly recommend agreeing to the terms and signing the contract," Mike says. "Who else knows about this?" he asks.

"You for right now. I had already gone over it and was pretty sure that I wanted to go ahead and sign it, but I thought it would be prudent of me to have an attorney, i.e. you to look over it. Now with that being said, yes I am really thinking about moving and no I do not want to discuss this any further. I have another reason for coming over here," Asia replies.

"Mike, I know you are hurting and I know that you are also pissed, but you and Leslie need to talk," Asia says.

"A, you know how long I have been saying I wanted to slow down and start a family. I have let a lot of Leslie's ways go because she's my wife and I love her, and I am not perfect by any means. But this, this was one of the most selfish things she has ever done. Then she called me over to the house under the pretense that there was some sort of emergency, which then proceeded with her giving me some ultimatum to come home or else!" Mike exclaimed. "Now, we both know demanding anything out of me will never work, but what pissed me off is she still has not apologized.   Not to mention, she got Kyle all caught in it. But not before insinuating that Kyle and I had something going on. Here I am thinking I did something wrong by going to talk with her about an argument Leslie and I had. Thinking, am I too familiar with you all? I felt so bad, and then I find out Leslie's pregnant and didn't tell me? Come on Asia, you know that is just foul.

I love Leslie with all that I have, but she's selfish, and I do not know if she can change. She wasn't always like this, Les used to be so chill, so thoughtful, and funny. Once our business increased, she became more interested in work than being my wife. I get it we got busy, but I remembered every birthday, Valentine's Day, anniversary, and just because flowers and gifts. You, Kyle and Evian drilled into me not to get too busy to be a good man, and what good did it do me?" he expressed. "I have done all I can do, at this point the ball is in Les' court. I am not going to make any special provisions for her when she can't even muster up an apology for what she did wrong! So if you came here to talk me into letting it go and moving back to the house, you should've just scanned the contract over and saved your time," Mike finishes.

"First, no, I didn't come here to ask you to get over it and go home," Asia explains. "I really did want you to review the contract in person and tell me your thoughts, but I also wanted to check in on you. We are more than friends, we're family. I also wanted to offer to facilitate the conversation between you two so that each person hears what the other has to say. Is that cool with you?" she asks.

"Of course, I'm open to that," Mike says.

"Perfect!" Asia grabs her phone out of her purse and texts Leslie.

> Asia: Come over to the condo. Mike and I are here and ready to talk.
> Leslie: I am on my way, give me 10 minutes.

"What was all that about?" Mike asks.

"Oh, Leslie is on her way she will be here in ten minutes," Asia responds.

"Hold up! what?! A, I didn't know you meant today," Mike says.

"What exactly are we waiting for? You are open to talk. Les is available. Let's rip this bandaid off today. Whatever happens after is what it is, but the bandaid comes off today brotha," Asia says, winking and toasting her almost empty glass in the air. "Now, pour me another glass of wine and get a bottle of Perrier out of the fridge for Les, please and thank you."

"I can't believe you, you're a trip," Mike says, as he walks to the kitchen and grabs the bottle of wine from the counter and a bottle of Perrier from the fridge.

"Oh and FYI, my contract has no public or girlfriend knowledge just yet," Asia reminds Mike, making a zip your lip gesture with her hands.

"Duh, I figured that shit out already A," Mike replies.

As Mike and Asia sit on the sofa and talk, the elevator door opens, and Leslie walks in.

"Hey Les," Asia says as she gets up from the couch to give Leslie a hug. "How are you feeling?" Asia asks.

"A little tired, but I am good," Leslie responds.

"Do you want something to eat or drink Les?" Mike asks.

"No, actually I am going to use the restroom. My bladder feels like it's going to burst," Leslie responds walking toward the bathroom.

When Leslie walks out of the bathroom a few minutes later, she sits on the love seat across from Mike and Asia.

"Well, you both know why we are here, so I'm going to start by saying you both need to have open ears, hearts, and minds during this conversation, otherwise it's a waste of time. Please do not interrupt the other nor devalue the others perception of a situation. I love you both and I am here for you both. With that being said who would like to start?" Asia asks.

"I will start," Leslie says. "I want to first say, Mike, I heard everything you said the last time we spoke. You were absolutely right. I have been selfish, I had not taken your feelings into consideration. But I swear I was not going to have an abortion. I was scared, I didn't know how being pregnant was going to affect my ability to work, because honestly that has taken center stage. Telling Kyle wasn't planned, it kind of came out. We had just had a fight, and I literally found out that morning shortly after you left."

Mike takes a deep breath, but before he could say anything, Asia puts her hand up and points to Leslie.

"Keep going Les," Asia says.

"The truth is, I know how terrible of a job I've been doing as your wife, and I wasn't sure and still am not sure I will make a good mom. Mike you have no idea how sorry I am for not just the baby, but for forgetting that you needed me the same way I needed you. For forgetting that we are a team. I got so caught up in business, it's like I forgot how to be both the other half of a thriving law firm and your wife. It's crazy because I remember when we first told our friends and family that we were going to start our own firm, they thought that working together and living together would eventually become too much. Maybe subconsciously I bought into that and purposely created space so that wouldn't happen and ended up missing in action. For that I am so sorry," Leslie apologizes, tears now streaming down her face.

Mike motions to get up, but Asia puts her hand up again.

"Have a seat Mike, you need to say your peace now, because we all know that you bottle things up until you burst," Asia says as she reaches in her purse and takes some tissues out. She walks over and sits by Leslie and puts her arm around and gives her the tissues.

"Okay Mike, the floor is yours," Asia says.

"Leslie, that's all I really wanted all this time. For you to acknowledge what you did hurt me and apologize for it. As far as you being a good mom is concerned, I have never once doubted your ability to be a great mother. Leslie, no matter what we've been through I have always been able to see you. That's why I really didn't make waves over some of the " things you did prior to the baby incident. Because I know the woman I married. I knew eventually I would get her back, but when you didn't tell me about the baby, I started thinking maybe I was wrong. Maybe the woman I knew and took vows with was really gone, and that's why I left. It was the hardest decision I ever had to make, to leave my pregnant wife. Man this shit killed me. You don't know how many times I wanted to come to the house to stay, but I just couldn't get over what you did," Mike explains.

"Mike, I never meant to hurt you the way I did, nor did I mean to make you feel like you were in this marriage alone. Do you think you can forgive me?" Leslie asks.

"Les, you are my right and left hand, of course I can."

Leslie gets up and walks over to Mike, who stands up and embraces her for what seems like hours.

"And Les, I want to apologize for being gone so long. I–" Leslie puts her finger over his lips.

"I just want us to go home, is that okay?" Leslie asks.

"Yes babe, that's okay."

Mike looks over at Asia.

"A, what can I say? Thank you. I love you," Mike says.

"Asia–"

"Okay, enough of all the mushy talk, I get it, I'm amazing," Asia says smiling, cutting Leslie off.

They break out into laughter.

"That's your friend," Mike says to Leslie kissing her on her forehead.

"No buddy, that's your sister," Leslie responds jokingly.

"No, but seriously guys, I'm glad I could help. I love you both so much, seeing you both hurting was really hard for me. When are you going to let Kyle off the hook? You know she was just trying to be a good friend to both you," Asia says.

"Babe, Asia is telling the truth. Kyle was just trying to be a good friend, you know she would never betray you," Leslie agreed.

"I know, I know. I will talk to her, I promise, but for now can we get some food? I'm starving," Mike says.

Now you're speaking my language: food!" Asia says.

"Let's go to that new Italian place downtown. And here I thought I was supposed to be the greedy one," Leslie says laughing.

Chapter 18
Changes...

"Asia, your phone has been going off for the past two hours, are you going to answer it?" Kyle asks.

"Girl no, that's Keith. I know why he's calling and I am not interested in talking to him about my business," Asia responds, switching the phone to silent.

"Okay, but what happened? And why is he calling like today is his last day on earth?"

"Well, you know I've been talking about how I really want to quit working at the spa and branch off on my own, right? So, I think I may have a business proposition that will allow me to purchase a house that is big enough for me to teach my classes, live in, and not go broke trying to pay the mortgage," Asia explains.

"Oh wow! That is great news! Have you signed a contract?" Leslie asks.

"Not yet, I am still mulling it over," Asia says.

"Are you worried about clientele A? You will be fine, your classes at the spa stay overbooked, and you already have super loyal clients. You will be rolling in the dough before you know it," Kyle says winking at her.

"I don't know. I have a good thing going at the spa, what if I am being ungrateful for what I do have? What if I fail?" Asia responds.

"Failure is not an option. You have made the spa tons of money, maybe it's time to write up two business plans, one showing how you have and continue to make the company money and would like to be an investor, and another for this potential business venture, in the event that the spa doesn't see how valuable you are?" Leslie suggests.

"She's right A. If the spa cannot see your worth, maybe it's time to go. You are always telling us that the universe makes no mistakes. Well, it's time to take your own advice," Kyle says.

"I am still confused as to how this opportunity and Keith coincide," Leslie says.

"His agent is the person who presented this opportunity to me, and I'm assuming he must have mentioned it to Keith. But I really don't want to talk about that until I have made a decision. I need my mind clear to think this through carefully. Is that okay?" Asia asks.

"Of course, we totally understand," Leslie says.

"So, Ms. DeBrow, I saw Patrick pulling up to your house pretty late the other night. Are you two working things out? Are you going to accept his proposal?" asks Asia.

"Wow! Thanks for putting me on blast, 'Celebrity Stalker', Kyle says sarcastically. "I asked him to come over to talk. I really wanted to know what prompted this change of heart.

"I personally think it was a money issue. I think he wanted to feel you guys were on an even playing field. Because the ink is barely dry on that deal he signed and now here he comes," Leslie says.

"No girl, I think seeing you at that event with Leo is the cause," Asia says.

"His side of the story is a little bit of both. He said he felt like he couldn't keep up with my lifestyle, and when he saw me he realized he handled our relationship cowardly and irresponsibly. He apologized and asked that I just think about it. So I am thinking about it," Kyle says.

The room goes silent.

"I still cannot believe that Leo was involved in Evian's story of being asked to step down," Kyle says, quickly changing the subject.

"I know, he seemed like such a good guy. How are you taking it? Wait, Kyle please don't tell me you are thinking about this Patrick thing because of what happened with you and Leo," Asia says.

"I'm fine. And no, he has nothing to do with it. Leo is dead to me, what he did is unforgivable. That is totally separate from Patrick," Kyle responds sharply.

"Well, my vote is still no, Kyle. Marriage is work and his track record has been to run or do a disappearing act when things get rough. I'm not saying you are going to say yes, I'm just giving you something to ponder on," Leslie says.

"I just want to see this ring in person, and I know you have it so let's see it Kyle," Asia says.

"You don't know me," Kyle responds laughing and rolling her eyes. She reaches into her purse, pulls out a ring box and hands it to Asia.

"Dammit, this thing is flawless! He did not come to play! But I agree, it feels like he has something to prove and it has more to do with what he can give you. My vote is no," Asia says.

"Thank you both for your votes, but this one I have to figure out on my own, Kyle states."

"Understood. "Okay, I need to get home to my husband," Leslie says as she gets up from the recliner.

"Yes, I have to be making my exit as well. Thanks for inviting us over A," Kyle says.

"Of course! I'm so glad you both came over. Oh, here girl, don't forget your ring," Asia says handing over the ring box.

Kyle throws the box back into her purse saying, "I can't wait to hear about what you've decided regarding whether you're going to stay or leave the spa. I believe any decision you make will be the best one, but I vote to leave and get your own," Kyle says as she kisses Asia on the cheek and walks out the door.

"I concur," Leslie says. "We are always rooting for you girl. Whatever you decide, I am team Asia. Do whatever your soul tells you to do."

As Leslie is waddling out, Tangi is walking into the apartment.

"Hey big mama, how are you feeling?" Tangi asks.

"Like a stuffed turkey," Leslie replies smiling at her.

"Get home safe, text me when you get home please so I know you arrived safely," Tangi says.

"Yes Mother," Leslie replies as she gets into her car.

"Hey A."

"Hey Tan, how was your day?" Asia asks.

"Before we talk about my day, can we talk about something else?" Tangi asks.

"Okay," Asia says in a skeptic tone.

"It's not bad or confrontational girl, calm down," Tangi reassures as she grabs a bottle of champagne out of the fridge, pops the cork and pours two glasses..

"Okay, this must be good news since you grabbed the champagne," Asia replies. "Asia, I owe you an apology," Tangi says as she takes a seat on the sofa and sets the two champagne flutes on the table.

"Admitting I am wrong is not my greatest gift. I know that I have been really selfish and ungrateful. You have helped me so much and I literally acted like a fucking asshole. I don't even know how you deal with some of the stunts I pull. I am ashamed of myself, because you did nothing to warrant that crazy behavior. I think I just got so used to always getting my way, I got crazy with it. Please accept my apology," Tangi says.
Asia, now in full blown tears, says "Of course I accept your apology! Now tell me about your day because clearly you have good news."

"Well, since you ask," Tangi says with a huge smile, topping up both her and Asia's glasses. "I was sitting in my studio last week literally in tears trying to figure out how I was going to make this whole clothing line happened, when Helena called. And I remembered she had called me before about a potential investor. At the time she called I felt like the investor was asking a lot of me, but I got over that really quick when she called the second time and thankfully they were still interested in investing. So I worked on all of the things the investor wanted and submitted them via Helena."

"Wait, so who were they and did you have a chance to meet with them to discuss your terms and theirs, etc?" Asia asks.

"That's a good question. I asked and Helena said they would send me a contract with all that information and then I could look them up. So, two things happened today while I was at the studio. First, Helena stopped by with what I thought would be the contract. Instead, she hands me an envelope. I open it and there's a check inside for $200,000. I look up at Helena, and before I could say anything she says, 'No darling, this is not from me but from someone who believes in your work. They asked for all of the paperwork you sent in to ensure you were serious and had a plan,'" Tangi explains.

"Do you have any idea who it could be?" Asia asks.

"Honestly, I don't," Tangi says as she shrugs her shoulders. "Okay, onto part two of the day. It has good news and bad news, which version would you like to hear first?"

"I will take the good news," Asia says.

"I got offered my own reality/styling show!!!"

"Shut up?!" Asia screams, clasping her hands over her mouth. "How could there possibly be bad to go with that?" she asks.

"Well, I would have to relocate to New York. They want to film there," Tangi says.

"Oh wow! How do you feel about that?" Asia asks.

"Even though I am a born and raised California girl and I will miss LA, I feel like New York has always been good to me. I got my first job, client, and met all my ride or die girls there," Tangi explains.

"Tan, this is exciting news, I'm so happy and proud of you. So when is this big move supposed to happen?"

"Well, I have 3 to 4 months to get myself settled and moved to start filming the pilot. I am thinking of pushing the grand opening back so I can incorporate it into the show for better exposure, so that in the event it doesn't get picked up for more than one season, people will still know who I am and that I have a clothing line," Tangi replies.

"That's actually a really good idea. I am so happy for you!" Asia says in excitement. "I also have some news that I haven't shared with anyone except Mike. I felt like since we live together and share the bills you should be the first to hear it."
Asia takes a deep breath.

"So Keith's manager emailed me and asked if we could meet about a possible opportunity for me. Now, I thought he was full of it, and that Keith was just trying to weasel his way back into my life, because I'm not an athlete. But I went ahead and met with him. So, one of Keith's teammates who used to have private yoga and mediation sessions at the spa for his wife and himself wants to open a wellness studio catered towards athletes," Asia explains. "He said he was looking for someone who knew the business to go in 50/50 with him. He would be a silent partner and I would basically have full control of the design, the classes, everything. The only stipulation is that it's in Bali. I also will have to move and be gone I imagine for two years. It will take that long to get the business to a place where it can run on its own and I can release the day to day running of the business to someone else and then just focus on teaching classes when and if I want. I had Mike review the contract terms, but even before he looked it over, I knew I was going to take the opportunity. So I signed papers and had Mike send them to his manager yesterday. I wanted to tell you first because I didn't want to leave you hanging with all the bills," Asia explains.

"That is fucking fantastic! But damn, two whole years? I am beyond excited for you, but I won't lie, I'm going to miss you so much. But hell, now I can just visit you in Bali, and since I have never been there, I now have the perfect reason to go. Okay, let's finish this bottle and have a roomie celebratory dinner!" Tangi says.

"Yes! I'll drink to that," Asia says, raising her glass in the air. "

Tan, What's the name of your company again?"

"What I Wear LLC, why?"

"I think I know who invested in your company. I don't know if you'll be happy or mad about it," Asia explains.

"Who? Tell me!"

"I think it might be Kyle," Asia says.

"Kyle?! What makes you think it's her? She's still pissed at me. I tried to invite her to lunch, but she declined about a week ago," Tangi replies.

"Well, she must have forgiven you because I was sitting in Kyle's office earlier this week having a 'working lunch' as she calls it and I saw a check for that exact amount just lying on her desk. I only remember because I asked why wasn't it in a safe or something and she said that someone was coming to pick it up. And that's who it was made out to," Asia explains.

Tangi places her hand over her mouth, "I can't believe she would do something so generous, even after I've been such a bitch to her. Are you sure A? Like positive?"

"Only one way to find out," Asia responds. Picking up her phone, she places the phone on speaker and calls Kyle.

"Hello?" Kyle's voice comes from out the other speaker.

"Hey babe, I have a question. Remember that check I saw on your desk earlier this week? Was it to invest in Tan's business?" Asia asks.

"You really are secret squirrel, but yes. Please do not tell her, I don't want her to think I thought she was some charity case. Helena and I were having lunch and she told me about the original investor backing out, and I do believe in her, I just want her to be more present and take care of business. So I cooked up this story that an investor was interested given she sends in a business plan along with other provisions. I needed to know she would put in the work before I wrote out the check. And she did! I want her to succeed and be great! You better not let this information leave your lips," Kyle demands.

"I am not going to say a word," Asia says.

"Okay girl, I have to go. I have some loose ends to tie up here at work," Kyle says.

"As usual, never home always working. Okay, and you know you are the bomb right?" Asia says, looking directly at Tangi.

I am something, I'll call you later.

"Okay, love you girl," Asia says as she ends the call.

Tangi is sitting in shock.

"Tan, you know what you have to do, now don't you?" Asia asks.

"Yeah, I do."

Chapter 19

Flipping the Script... Evian

Kyle: Hey Evian, are you home? I need to talk to you, it's an emergency!

Evian: I'm home! Come on over, is everything okay?

Kyle: I am pulling up to your garage now.

Evian walks to the door to open it for Kyle.
"Hey girl, what's wrong?" Evian asks.
"Everything! I have been trying to catch up with you for the last two days, but you haven't been responding to my calls or texts," Kyle says.
"I know, I'm sorry. I needed to take a timeout. I'm working on something and needed to focus all my attention on it. But you know you can always just come over," Evian replies.
"I know how that snake Jake, got those pictures of you and Phil, as well as you and Steele and Clarke," Kyle says.
"How?" Evian asks surprised.

"Leo, that's how! A couple of days ago, the same night I got the surprise proposal. He and I were about to head out, and he told me. He said that there was something he needed to tell me, and that it had been weighing on his heart for a while. When I asked what was wrong, he told me that he and Jake were frat brothers and Jake asked him to take the pictures. When I asked him how he could do something like that, he tried to plead his case and say that Jake had made the impression that you had underhandedly stolen the partnership from him and he was just helping him get it back. He said he had no idea that Jake was going to do what he did what the pictures until Jake accidentally told on himself. I am enraged!!! Oh, and he said you're assistant was in on it as well.

"Now that part I do know. The day they gave me the 'talk' Jacks assistant asked me to meet her for lunch, and she spilled all the beans. But boy, do I have a trick up my sleeve for them. We meet this afternoon to. I am supposed to tell them whether I have decided to accept the terms of the separation agreement or not," Evian explains.

"Oh girl! What's the trick up your sleeve?" asks Kyle.

"Jake thought he was being strategic and smart using my assistant to do his bidding, but guess what? Little Jake doesn't know that firm is in a financial crisis of their own. Hence, why they voted me in as partner, I bring in the most revenue. Once Jake's backstabbing scheme began, Jack and Phil assumed they would close the Steele and Clark merger without me. However, before I accepted the partnership I was already approved for a loan to start my own firm, I just didn't have the staff to pull off the project. But with the recent turn of events at the firm, I have received numerous calls and emails from not just the firm's current agents, but Steele and Clarke's along with upcoming agents in the industry who all want to know my next move. Every one of them have stated that wherever I decide to go they would like the opportunity to work with me."

"Evian, that is amazing! You are sure making waves now!" Kyle exclaims.

"And as far as Steele and Clarke is concerned, no deal for the prestigious firm of Hunter, Hoffman, and Associates," Evian continues. "They have decided that it is in their best interest to merge with a boutique agency that can service both their sports clientele as well as their entertainment clientele."

"Do tell, what boutique agency would that be?" Kyle asks smiling from ear to ear.

"Well, I guess I might as well spill it. As of 3pm this afternoon, approximately five minutes after my meeting is scheduled to end, an announcement will be made to the general public. Steele and Clark has been purchased and will be merging with The Graham Management Group, their full roster of clients have already signed new contracts with said boutique agency," Evian states proudly. "Since the terms in my separation agreement say nothing about a non-compete, I am safe from any and all litigation as per my attorney."

"That's my girl!" Kyle says. "How did you manage the deal with Steele and Clarke?" Kyle asks.

"They only wanted to do business with Hunter and Hoffman because I was there, meaning no me, no deal. That's the part I left out when I spoke with Phil."

"Oh my god! To be a fly on the wall when they find out there will be no merger and most of their staff and clients will be departing," Kyle says.

"I already have the office space, and I'm almost fully staffed. That's why I have been M.I.A. I had to get all the loose ends tied before today's meeting and press conference."

"I am so proud of you E!" Kyle says.

"I know they thought I was going to take their little $150,000 check and go crazy trying to find a firm to hire me. Joke's on them now and that money is going to furnish my new office. You think I should send a fruit basket saying thank you?" Evian asks sarcastically.

"Maybe a fruit basket to Phil and Jack and flowers to Jake and Todd, no card attached," Kyle says laughing.

"So what happened between you and Leo?" Evian asks, changing the subject.

"Oh, I basically told him I never wanted to see him again, that he was a snake just like his buddy, and to stay the hell away from me. I should have known something was up when he asked me how long we had been friends and how long you have been in the Sports Management world. I assumed he was just making small talk, cause he asked about all the girls. But clearly he was covering up his true intentions. What a piece of shit," Kyle says.

"Calm down Kyle. Neither Jake nor Leo can damage my reputation. I worked hard to earn it, the loyalty that has been shown speaks for itself.

"I know, but it still bothers me that neither had any regard for you as a person. Makes me want to let rats loose in his tired ass restaurant," Kyle says.
Evian burst into laughter, "That would be awesome, but we're not going to do that because I am good," Evian says.

"I am so glad. You really have flipped the script on those assholes. I know you have to prepare for your meeting so I will leave you to it and keep my phone notifications on," Kyle says as she gives Evian a big hug and walks out the apartment.

"Okay girl, I love you and thanks for always looking out for me," Evian says.

Evian closes the front door, walks into her bedroom and goes into the closet.

"Hmm…what to wear?" she says to herself smiling.

She pulls out a white blazer, white slacks and red blouse from her closet, and grabs her leopard pumps off the shelf.   As she walks out of the door to her car, she receives an email on her phone from Steele and Clarke confirming the contract has been signed and executed. Evian dances in her seat listening to the radio with the top down on her convertible. She pulls up to the valet in the garage of Hunter, Hoffman, and Associates.

Evian walks directly into the conference room, "Well, gentleman," she states to Jack and Phil. "I have had the time to have my attorney go over the separation agreement terms. I am in total agreement that this separation is in the best interest of both the company and myself. I wish that things had gone in a different direction. I am highly disappointed in the both of you, as it has always been my mission to make this firm the biggest and best in the country, and for you both to question my integrity is a huge insult. I do, however, wish you luck in your future endeavors and I am sure we will cross paths in the future, where I hope we can do so professionally and cordially. I received the email with regards to the Steele & Clarke deal, but it would be remiss of me to not inform you that I have heard through the grapevine that there is another small firm reaching out to them proposing a merger and/or buyout."

"We thank you Evian, but we are quite confident that there is not another firm with our high track record of success. We have already reached out to the contact listed in the email you sent to Phil," Jack says.

"Evian, I hope there are no hard feelings. You have been a tremendous asset to this firm and its success," Phil says.

"Hard feelings? No, absolutely not. This was business, not personal," Evian replies as she signs the agreement and pushes it toward Jack.

Both Jack and Phil read and sign the agreement, sliding it back to her along with her severance check.

Evian places the check in her purse, and with a big smile she says, "It has been my pleasure working for this firm and again I wish you the best of luck," Evian says extending her hand to Jack.

Jack shakes Evian's hand

"I am so glad we were able to resolve this amicably," Phil says, next in line to shake Evian's hand.

"So am I," Evian says and walks out of the conference room.

Jessica, Jack's longtime assistant, walks into the conference room.

"Mr. Hunter, I just wanted to submit my letter of resignation," Jessica says handing him a letter.

"Jessica, what's this about?" Jack asks.

"I have decided to just move on and explore my options with another company," Jessica explains. "Oh, and you may want to check your email, it appears several of the agents are resigning as well," she says as she walks out the door.

Jack opens his laptop and sees several emails with 'Letter of Resignation' in the subject line.

"Jack, have we just lost some our best agents?" Phil asks.

"Get Jake in here and see where he is with the Steel and Clarke deal, we may not need them any longer, Jack replies.

Phil texts Jake to come into the conference room, and within 30 seconds, Jake walks into the conference room.

"Have a seat Jake, Phil says.

"So where are we on the Steele and Clarke deal? Have they agreed to the terms in our contract?" Jack asks.

Before Jake can reply, all the gentlemen receive a text from an unknown number.

Unknown: Late breaking news: Please click on link.

"This must be some sort of spam," Phil says putting his phone down.

Immediately they receive another text from the same unknown number.

Unknown: Checkmate: Click link below

"What the hell is going on?!" Jack yells.

"Goddammit!" Phil yells.

"What?" Jack asks.

"Apparently Steel and Clarke have decided to do business with The Graham Management Group!" Phil says showing Jack a press release update on his phone.

Under a picture of Evian in the same outfit she was wearing during the meeting is the headline, *The Golden Lady of Sports Management Strikes a Major Deal!*

"You are fucking shitting me!" Jack says.

"No, and since we did not include any non-compete verbiage in her separation agreement, we have no recourse," Phil says.

"Wait, I can fix this. Let me make a call," Jake says.

"Enough!" Jack says. "Call the state unemployment benefits department, because you are fired!"

Chapter 20
Paris is calling….

Kyle walks into her office to find a huge box wrapped in pink wrapping paper and a beautiful white bow on the loveseat on the other side of the room. She stands halfway out the door and sees that Bethany is not at her desk.

Damn, I can't even ask Bethany where this came from.

She carefully unravels the bow and opens the box. In it she finds a large pink manila envelope, with "Great News' written on the front. She opens a second envelope with what appears to be a card in it. A card with a family sitting at a table having a drink is on the cover. The card reads:

Dear Kyle,
You have been more than my home girl and my sister for as long as I can remember. There would never be an opportunity where you didn't have my back, and it felt like even though you knew it was wrong you chose

Leslie's side and didn't have my back. I reacted badly is an understatement. I wasn't sure how to say I'm sorry, then something came to me. Look in the pink envelope. - Mike

Kyle opens the envelope and pulls out a cardboard mockup of the magazine cover that says FBNK Paris. There was another note:

That's right, Paris is calling. They want to set up an FBNK office and the French version of your magazine sis. I hope this makes up for my bullshit. I am so proud of you. Leslie and I want to be the first to say congratulations!

Kyle immediately starts jumping up and down.

"Yes! Yes! Paris, I am coming for you!" Bethany walks in.

"Ms. DeBrow, is everything okay?"

"Okay? Everything is awesome!" Kyle says as she flips the cardboard markup over and shows it to Bethany. Bethany's eyes go wide in surprise.

"Oh my god! We're starting a French version of the magazine?" Bethany asks.

"Yes, we are! I have to make a call, but we will have a lot of work to do, so block off two hours today to meet with me so we can go over some of the logistics."

"Yes ma'am," Bethany says and walks back to her desk.. Kyle picks up the phone at her desk and starts dialing.

"I take it that we're cool and all is forgiven?" Mike's voice says through the receiver.

"Mike, is this for fucking real?!

"Yes, it is. They reached out to me about a month ago and I didn't like the original terms of the contract. You would not have had enough creative control over the magazine, and I knew you would not agree, so I told them try again and get back to me. Well, last week I received a revised version of their terms. I made some notes and sent it back, and they agreed to my changes and sent it right back to me the same day, signed and ready to execute. All you have to do is come by the office or I can come there and you can look it over and see if you want to change anything and sign on the dotted line," Mike replies.

"What's the timeline look like?"

"I think they already have the office space so you will need to fly out there and conduct a walk-through and see if you need any construction work done and discuss the design of the office. So, it's looking like about 6 to 9 months for everything. That includes any construction, designing, furnishing and staffing of the office. However, you will have to be there within the next month to discuss the logistics," Mike says.

"Okay, I'll come over to your office later this afternoon to go over the contract, if that works for you," Kyle says.

"Yeah, how about around 3:30pm?" Mike asks.

"That's perfect. See you then. And for the record, yes we are cool and all is forgiven," Kyle says.

"I figured as much. I'll see you later," Mike says.

Kyle hangs up the phone and picks up the cardboard markup gazing at it smiling.

"FBNK Paris," she says to herself.

Kyle places the picture on the table and walks over to her desk.

"*Oh my God my focus is all off. I have so much to do today,*" she thinks to herself. Bethany walks in as Kyle replies to emails.

"Hey boss lady. You ready to meet?" she asks.

"Yes, come on in and have a seat, so I spoke with Mike McCall and he has confirmed that there is a contract on the table for us to expand. We'll be setting up an office similar to ours here, which will mean we will need a full staff. So far, the timeline for the office to be fully staffed and operational is 6 to 9 months, and I will have to start preparing to leave to go there within the next month.

"How's your French? Because I am going to need you to come with me to Paris, there is a lot to be done, and I am going to need you there," Kyle explains.

"My French is very good, thanks to you sending me to those French classes last year," Bethany replies.

"Great, we have tons of interviews to conduct so it will be imperative that your French is more than fluent. We also will need to perform a walk-through of the building itself and determine if any construction work will need to be done. I would really like it to be a mirror image of the office here, if possible. Oh, and then at some point you will need to help me hire a new assistant," Kyle says.

"Oh yes, for the Paris office, absolutely," Bethany replies.

"No, for this office. Well, that's if you are interested in a promotion, Kyle hints. "I will need a VP of operation for the Paris office and I can't think of anyone that I trust more and that is more qualified than you. I will be between our satellite office in New York and our headquarters here, so the likeliness of my being in Paris on a full time basis is slim. I need someone who knows the ins and outs of the magazine and can lead the operations in a manner that models what we have being doing in New York and here in LA. So, I guess among the many other interviews you will have to help me with, you will have to interview for two assistants, yours and mine," Kyle says in a very nonchalant manner. The room goes quiet.

"Wait, are you serious?" Bethany says, trying to hold back the excitement in her voice.

"As a heart attack. You have worked hard and learned a lot, and didn't you recently get your MBA? I know it has seemed like I have pushed you to your breaking points sometimes and that I put a lot on your plate, but I feel like it is my job to bring the best out of you, because I knew you would one day need to spread your wings and fly. And if you are going to be as great as I think you can be, I want you to flourish with us. That is, if you want the job."

"I…I don't even know what to say," Bethany says, speechless.

"Well, I hope you're going to say you want the job."

"Yes! Of course! I definitely want the job. Thank you so much! I promise I will not let you down.

"I am positive you won't," Kyle replies. "Okay, so let's get to work. I have a meeting with Mike, and you should definitely come so you can be in the loop from the start. Can you be ready to leave here in about ten minutes? Kyle asks.

"Yes ma'am," Bethany answers.

"Also, once I have reviewed the contract and signed it, let's get with HR to post your job. I will notify them that you have been promoted and will work with them to get your new job description ready so your pay can be adjusted to reflect your new role ASAP."

"Yes ma'am," Bethany says.

"One last thing, there will be no more calling me ma'am. Call me Kyle or Kylisha, whichever you choose if fine with me. Finally, please find me another you," Kyle says, with her hands in a praying position.

"I will try my best," Bethany replies.

****

Kyle pulls into the garage at Leslie and Mike's law firm. She and Bethany walk into the reception area.

"Good afternoon, Ms. DeBrow. Mr. and Mrs. McCall are expecting you. They are in Conference room A," the receptionist says, pointing down the hall. As they enter into the conference room, Kyle sees a medium sized pink box on the table sitting in front of Leslie.

"Good afternoon Mrs. McCall," Kyle says, as she takes a seat across from Leslie.

"Good afternoon, Kyle. Mike is on his way in with the paperwork. We reviewed the documents very carefully and we both think you will be happy with the terms of the contract," Leslie says smiling.

"Great, so what's in the box?" Kyle asks.

"Nothing you need to be bothered with at this moment. Just then, Mike walks in with a folder. He takes a seat and pushes the folder across the table to Kyle.

"Do you want some time to review the paperwork alone?" Mike asks.
Kyle flips through page after page.

"I cannot believe this is for real," She says, as she flips to the last page. "You both were right, these terms are amazing! Someone give me a pen, I am ready to sign!" As Kyle signs the contract, Leslie opens the pink box and pulls out a cake with the same design on it that was on the markup. It reads: 'Congratulations Kyle we are so happy for you!'

"Thank you so much! There is no way this would have happened without you. I am truly blessed to have not just as my friends but

as my legal team. Now let's get into this cake!"
Kyle says.

Chapter 21

Save the date…

"I can't believe that it's been 4 months since you left Hunter and Hoffman. How have things been at the Graham Management Group?" Kyle asks.

"I know, time has flown by so quickly. Things are great actually. Forbes Magazine reached out to me to do an article on me and the company," Evian replies.

"Oh my God, that's exciting news!"

"I'm excited and nervous," Evian confesses.

"You will be fine. Once you get in your zone about how you got into Sports Management you will talk non-stop," Kyle assures her.

"I'm not sure if that is a compliment, but I'll take it," Evian says laughing.

"Thanks for picking me up and driving to the gender reveal/baby shower," Kyle says. "Well, it's not like you could've driven with all the boxes of presents you've brought," Evian replies.

"I know, and because I didn't know whether it was a girl or boy gift buying was extra complicated," Kyle replies.

"Can you believe it's already gender reveal/baby shower time? I am so excited for Les and Mike," Evian says.

"So am I. Mike has been sending pictures of him and Les, every single ultrasound, and them shopping for baby furniture. Between Mike and Asia and her photos of her new spa, her on the beach teaching a class, her chilling on the beach, I do not think I have any more space in my office for pictures," Kyle says.

"Did you receive an invite to Tangi's grand opening/show pilot taping?" Evian asks.

"I did," Kyle says. "Did you two ever make up officially?"

"You mean did she ever apologize? No. But to her credit, she did invite me to dinner, but I literally didn't have the time with all that I had to do to get to Paris," Kyle replies.

"Speaking of Paris, how are things coming along?" Evian asks.

"They are coming along, we are only 3 months in. Thankfully there wasn't much construction that needed to be done, but the design is taking longer than I had expected, so we are working like maniacs to get it done. Bethany has been working her tail off," Kyle explains.

"Oh yes, you gave her a huge promotion," Evian says.

"She deserves it and has been proving me right for making her my right hand.

"I'm glad we are getting to the venue a little early, I want to make sure the cake came out how I described it to the bakery," Evian says.

"Would you mind pressing down on the gas pedal? Geez, we've been driving for 20 minutes and the place is only 10 minutes away, for God sakes," Kyle says.

"I am not speeding through traffic like some people I know. You're the passenger, so I suggest you sit, be quiet, and enjoy the ride."

Kyle rolls her eyes, "Wake me up when we get there," she says sarcastically.

"Well, wake up because we are here," Evian says as they pull up to the venue valet. When they arrive there are two different carpets to walk down to enter the venue, one pink and one blue. A backdrop with baby McCall and pictures of Leslie and Mike on it made for a great photo op. Evian and Kyle pose to have their photo taken before walking into the venue.

Upon entering, the room is filled with extra-large pink and blue teddy bears, stacks of giant play blocks that say 'It's a boy!' and 'It's a girl!' in the same color scheme, drinks with pink and blue cotton candy toppings lined up at the bar, blue, pink and white balloons scattered all over the floor and hanging from the ceiling. The stage is decorated with a long table beautifully embellished with baby décor, complete with dramatically positioned white theater curtains to finish the themed look .

"Kyle!" Asia screams, running into the venue with her arms wide open.

"A!" Kyle screams back, her heels clacking on the floor as she runs towards Asia. The two hug for what seems like forever before Kyle backs up.

"Look at you! Bali looks good on you, girl. You let your hair grow out and now you're wearing those natural curls. You are still color by mood I see," referring to Asia's thick black curly hair with platinum blonde, pink and blue streaks.

"I had to look good for baby McCall of course" Asia says winking at Kyle.

"Where's Evian? I thought you two rode in together?"

"We did. She went to check on the cake."

"The diva has arrived!" everyone hears a voice yell from the doorway.

"Oh my God! Tan! Asia yells.

"Oh my god, A! You look fantastic! I mean seriously, but what is up with your hair? Looking like Diana Ross gone my little pony," Tangi says laughing.

"Don't hate!" Asia says as she embraces her.

"Tangi," Kyle says with her arms open wide, smiling.

They embrace, and Tangi grabs Kyle's hand.

"I am going to steal her for a minute," Tangi tells Asia..

"Okay, I'm gonna go indulge in one of these cotton candy drinks," Asia says playfully and walks away.

"Kyle, I just want to say two things. I am so sorry I wasn't a better friend and I know it was you."

"You know what was me? The investment money?"

"I kept trying to get to you before you left to talk, because I wanted to say thank you in person not via some long text or email. And not on the phone either" Tangi explains.

"Tan, I promise I wasn't dodging you, the whole Paris move just took every bit of time I had," Kyle replies. "But you are so welcome and I am so fucking proud of you! You will have to film an episode in Paris," Kyle says.

"Oh my God, I would love that! I have missed you so much! Tangi says.

"I've missed you too. All of you. I think we took for granted that we all lived in the same city and could hang out whenever we wanted," Kyle says.

"I know, I miss those brunches, dinners, and simply just drinking a glass of wine and watching movies with the girls," Tangi says.

"Your dining out tab must be sky high. God knows you can't cook," Kyle says laughing.

"Don't start," Tangi says giving her another hug.

As crowds of people start to flow into the venue, Evian and Asia walk up to Tangi and Kyle, cotton candy cocktails in tow for the group.

"Tangi!" Evian says in excitement, giving her a big hug and a kiss on the cheek.

"E!" Tangi yells. "It's so good to see you!"

"Let's go have a seat at our table, my feet are starting to hurt from all this standing," Asia says.

The ladies start making their way to their table, when music starts to play. It's Mike and Leslie's grand entrance as they walk in together, hand in hand. All the guests begin to cheer and give the parents-to-be a warm welcome.

Leslie, glowing and smiling from ear to ear, is dressed in a pink strapless dress and white bedazzled flip flops, and Mike is wearing a powder blue suit, white V-neck t-shirt, and white sneakers. They make their rounds around the room saying hello and giving hugs and handshakes to all of their guests. Their final stop is at the ladies table.

"Oh my God, Leslie! You look like a supermodel with a basketball under her dress! Did you even gain any weight? You look beautiful!" Kyle says.

"I feel huge, and my feet are so swollen I can only wear flip flops," Leslie says, raising her right leg up to show the group. I am so ready for this baby to come on out!

"You look so good, you look no where near 8 months pregnant Leslie!" Evian says standing up from the table and hugging her tight.

"Is this pink and blue hair for us?" Mike asks Asia.

"Of course it is. I have to look good for baby McCall. I mean, I am Godmother # 2," she says.

"Yes, you are," Leslie says laughing and holding her belly.

"You two are #teamtoomuch. A blue and a pink carpet? It's cute, but I never thought you two would go so overboard, that's usually my department," Tangi says sipping on her pink cotton candy mimosa.

"That's all Mike's doing," Leslie explains. "I wanted to stop at the food and balloons. But he wasn't having it."

"You're damn right! Baby boy or girl McCall deserves all of it and more," Mike says with a big smile, kissing Leslie on her forehead.

"Well ladies, enjoy the festivities. We have to go up on stage and sit with our parents. We will check back in later" Leslie says.

"We love you guys and are so happy you are here," Mike says as they walk off towards the stage.

"So Asia, how are you loving Bali?" Evian asks.

"Guys, it is so wonderful! I get up whenever I want since classes are normally well after ten or eleven in the morning and I usually teach evening classes or late afternoon classes," Asia explains.

"I saw the video you sent us of the meditation class out on the ocean on the surf boards. That looks so freaking awesome!" Evian says.

"It's one of our most popular classes. We also do a yoga class on them," Asia says.

"Yoga?! Are you serious? I would literally bust my ass if I tried that class," Kyle laughs.

"That's half the fun! If you fall, you fall. No pressure and you get cooled off by the water from the hot sun," Asia says.

"No wonder you are so tanned," Tangi says, "It looks good on you girl. I would love to try that class, I'm not scared to fall."

"Well good, cause that's exactly what's going to happen," Kyle says laughing.

"We should all go for a week," Evian says.

"Count me out, I have zero time to take off," Kyle says.

"Count me out also. I am booked and busy," Tangi says.

"Well damn, guess I'm going alone," Evian laughs, raising her glass to the ladies. The conversation is interrupted by the sound of Mike's voice booming over the microphone. They all look towards the stage.

"I just want to thank everyone for coming and celebrating with Leslie and I. We are so excited and we can wait to meet baby boy or baby girl McCall. But as we were sitting at the table eating, Leslie said she's ready to know if it's a girl or a boy. Are you all ready?"

Everyone in the room screams a big "Yes!"

"I guess it's unanimous. Leslie, will you do the honors?" Mike says.

Leslie gets up from her chair and waddles towards a large gold rope attached to the white curtain.

Mike walks over and stands next to her. With the mic in hand, he starts to count, "One, two three!"

Leslie pulls the gold rope and the curtain comes down. In enormous billboard letters everyone screams "It's a girl!"

Balloons from the ceiling begin to pop as pink confetti starts to fall from out of them throughout the room.

Leslie and Mike give each other a big hug and kiss. Leslie takes the microphone from Mike, and says loud and clear, "Who runs the world?!" The crowd shouts back, "Girls!

"Who runs the world?!" she says again, and the crowd shouts again, "Girls!"

Now it's really time to party! Enjoy everyone!" Leslie says, as she puts the mic down and takes Mike's hand to walk down to the dance floor.

"Look at those two, reminds me of when they were in college, always lighting up the dance floor," Asia says.

"I know, right?! Those two were always the first and last on the dance floor back in college," Kyle says.

"I am so happy for them," Tangi says. "So E, who's the new beau? she asks, changing the subject.

"Whatever do you mean? What new beau?" Evian asks smiling from ear to ear.

"Bitch, don't play with us. You know who, the one that has been in every one of your Instagram posts for the past two months, that's who.

"The one you failed to mention on our various calls and group texts, that's who," Kyle adds.

"You are never going to believe this, but his name is Kyle. Crazy right? We met at a fundraiser in New York. He works in finance and lives on the upper west side.

"Oh! He lives in New York?" Tangi interrupts.

"Yes, he does. He's a good guy, but we are taking things slow," Evian says.

"Absolutely nothing wrong with taking things slow," Kyle says.

"Speaking of relationships, Kyle, I think you should hear Leo out and maybe give him a second chance. He only did what any of us would have done for the other if we were given the same amount of information that he was given," Evian says.

"Normally in these situations I am the first to say hell no! But I agree, Kyle. You know me in particular. I would have done the exact same for you or any of you all," Tangi says.

"Thank you both, but Leo is old news. It's been months and I haven't heard from him, so I will keep the status quo. After I told Patrick I wasn't going to marry him, nor was I going to consider the thought of us being together again, I decided to take a hiatus from dating. I am way too busy with not one, but two magazines. I do not have the bandwidth for a relationship right now. I barely have time for myself, let alone a whole other person," Kyle says.

"Kyle, you mean to tell me Leo never tried to call you?" Asia asks.

"Okay, I blocked his number, so I don't know," Kyle admits.

"I've taught you well. You never would block folks before, so I see you have gotten over that," Tangi says laughing.

All the ladies break into laughter.

"What are you girls over here giggling about?" Leslie says as she waddles over to their table and has a seat.

"Girl, nothing," Kyle says.

"A little girl. Are you excited?" Evian asks.

"I am, I am so happy," Leslie says with a smile that hasn't diminished once all day.

"She spoke her into existence, remember when we had dinner that time? She said we were starving her and her daughter," Asia laughs.

"Oh yeah, that's right!" Evian replies.

"I cannot wait to style that little baby girl up! Aunty Tan is gonna have that little girl looking like a mini diva!"

"Oh, don't I know it," Leslie replies laughing.

"It feels like forever since we were all together," Evian says.

"I know!" Asia says.

"Let's do dinner tomorrow," Leslie suggests.

"I'm in! I am here for two more days," Tangi says.

"I'm in too!" Asia says.

"I am definitely in!" Evian says.

"Fuck my life, I can't! I fly back to Paris tomorrow and then two days later I am in New York probably for about a month or two and then back home to LA," Kyle says.

"It's okay Kyle. We will relish in your presence today," Leslie says grabbing and squeezing her hand. "Now let's get on the dance floor before my feet hurt and I can't. I didn't get a DJ for nothing!"

Chapter 22

Au Revoir Paris, Hello Trouble

8am. Kyle, Bethany, the Art Department director, the Paris Editor in Chief, and the Chief Financial Officer, are sitting in the conference room of the Paris office. "Let's walk through the morning. I want to go over the remaining punch list of things we need to do before we start the launch of the first Paris issue. I also want to go over the details for the launch party. I will be returning to the states and working out of the NY satellite office for about a month or two. My Flight leaves at 11am so we do not have much time before I have to skip out of here, so let's get started," Kyle says.

The group goes over the current budget for the launch of the first issue and what else is needed in the office, with Bethany leading the discussions. By the time they get to the launch party portion of the meeting, Kyle interrupts.

"I hate to do this, but I am running so late. It's 10am and I can't miss my flight to New York. Can you all finish up without me, please? Just email me the details and I will email you back any questions or notes I have from the plane. But before I go, I want you all to know what a pleasure it has been to work with such a great group of professionals." Interrupted by the sound of a text coming in, Kyle checks her phone. She received a message from her new assistant Tammy, letting her know that the car service is still waiting for her. She quickly texts back that she is on her way down.

"That's my cue to get going. Au revoir ladies and gentleman!" she says as she runs out the door and onto the elevator.

Arriving at the airport at lightspeed, Kyle gets out of the car, checks in for her flight and gets through security to her gate just as they are boarding the first-class passengers. After boarding the plane and taking her window seat in first class, she pulls out her iPad, headphones, and cellphone out of her purse, switches them to airplane mode and sticks them in her purse. The flight attendant asks her if she would like anything to drink.

"Yes, a glass of champagne please," Kyle replies.

The flight attendant hands her a champagne flute filled to the top with bubbly. As she takes a sip, a man walks up to the seat across from her puts his luggage in the upper compartment. She looks up at the man.

"Leo?!" Kyle says, completely surprised by this encounter.

"Kyle?!" he says as he gets himself settled in his seat, which happens to be in the pod right next to hers. "It's been awhile," he says.

"Yeah, it has," Kyle replies.

"What are you doing in Paris? On vacation?" Leo asks.

"So much for sleep," Kyle thinks to herself. "No, we are actually setting up shop in Paris for our French version of the magazine," Kyle explains.

"Wow, that's amazing! Congratulations!"

"What about you? What brings you to Paris?" Kyle asks.

"Well, I got engaged about a week ago and was meeting my fiancé, who just opened up a restaurant here, and I came to show my support. Her name is Dina George."

"Oh, I've heard of her. She's an amazing chef. Congratulations! She's been in our magazine several times. Now that I think of it, we need some content for our first French issue. Do you think she would be interested in being featured in it?"

"Are you serious? Leo asks. Absolutely!"

"I love seeing women kicking ass and taking names," Kyle says smiling.

"I'm sure she would love it, but I will ask her to be sure," Leo replies.

"What about you? Are you dating anyone?" Leo asks.

"No, I'm still married to my career at the moment. I have not had the luxury of free time to have any sort of personal life."

"What about the ghost from Christmas past?" he says laughing.

"Well, I thought about it for a long time, and then decided to leave that ghost in the past, Kyle explains.

"I see you are headed to New York. Is that a connection or your destination?" Leo asks.

"He is still nosey as hell," Kyle thinks to herself. "It's my destination. We have a satellite office there and I will be working out of it for a few months," she replies.

"Okay cool, I'm in the process of opening a new restaurant and I will be in New York most likely until the end of the year. The plan is to have the grand opening on New Years eve."

"That's awesome! Congratulations," Kyle says genuinely.

The Captain alerts the stewardesses to prepare for takeoff. As the plane begins to take off, Kyle places a satin Tiffany blue eye mask over her eyes and puts her headset on and slowly drifts off to sleep. Leo follows suit and places his headset on and also dozes off to sleep. Several hours later, they are both awoken by the wheels of the jet landing on the tarmac.

"Do you have a ride home?" Leo asks.

"I'm just going to hop in a Lyft. I totally forgot to call the car service for a pickup."

"You don't have to get a Lyft. Where are you staying?"

"Oh um, I have a condo in Brooklyn."

"Okay, well, I actually have a car service picking me up. We can make a stop and bring you to your condo."

"Leo no, I don't want to put you out of your way."

"It's no trouble. I am staying at the Gansevoort hotel, it's only across the Brooklyn Bridge, and it will take me all of 15 mins to get to my hotel after dropping you off."

"Are you sure?" Kyle asks.

"I insist," Leo says.

"Okay, thank you."

They exit the plane and head to customs then to the baggage claim afterwards.

Kyle grabs her bags.

"Do you need help?" Leo asks.

"Thank you, but I'm good."

As they walk towards the ground transportation area, there is a well-dressed man in a black suit with a sign that says Leo Castellanos. Kyle and Leo get into a large black SUV as the driver places their luggage in the trunk. The driver gets into the SUV and starts the engine.

"We will be making a stop in Brooklyn," Leo says. What's your address Kyle?"

"Oh, I'm sorry, 150 Myrtle Avenue," Kyle replies loud enough for the driver to hear.

"You know Kyle. I wrote you several letters and you never responded to even one. I mean, I didn't expect you to forgive me, but I did want you to have a better understanding for why I did what I did. I finally got the picture that you just didn't want to hear from me.

That's a true and false statement. Yes, initially I was pissed and didn't care if I ever saw or heard from you again. The false part is I never received your letters. Anything that came to the house or office I had my new assistant Tammy, put it in a box for me and ship it to New York. I figured once I returned I could go through it all. Only packages were forwarded to me in Paris. And for the record, Leo, I forgive you. I won't lie to you, it took me a while, but I do understand why you did what you did."

"I am really glad to hear you say that," Leo says. Now can you unblock me so I can give you Dina's response to your offer once I speak to her? And yes, I know you blocked me," he says laughing.

Kyle laughs out loud.

"Yes, I can give your access back," she says, opening her phone and unblocks Leo's number. "See?" she shows him he is now unblocked.

"So tell me more about your restaurant. New York is home for me so I will need a nice spot to eat when I am here working," Kyle says.

"It's on 34th street and 14th Avenue, and I am thinking of making the menu more of a tapas style with some nice signature drinks. I have three months until the grand opening, so I will be running like a chicken with its head cut off till then," Leo says.

"Tapas, I like that. I am a small portions kind of a girl, so that most certainly works for me," Kyle says.

"It seems to me that these days most people like smaller portions with a larger variety of choice better," Leo says.

"Well, I am extremely happy for you." The SUV slows down and pulls up in front of a building.

"Is this you?" Leo asks.

"Yes sir, it is."

"Let me help you bring your bags up," Leo offers.

"You really don't have to," Kyle says. Leo gives her a 'please shut up' look and she allows him to grab her bags. They walk into the building and get into the elevator, Kyle pushing the PH button.

"Oh, penthouse huh? Aren't we fancy," Leo says laughing.

"Shut up," Kyle says smiling remembering how much she missed him making her laugh.

She quickly snaps out of it as the elevator doors open to her floor.

"Wow! This is really nice and your view is crazy. You can almost see the entire Manhattan skyline," Leo says as he helps Kyle bring her bags in.

"It's okay," Kyle replies in a very humble tone.

"What made you pick this place?" Leo asks.

"I. as you know, am a Brooklyn girl born and raised, so I wanted be and feel at home when I have to be here. The promenade has always been one of my favorite places to just sit and take in the city or to just think. And I am not too far away from it here. Many of my life decisions were made on the benches of the promenade you know," Kyle says smiling.

"That's really cool," Leo says.

"Well, I won't keep you. I know you have to get back to your hotel and get some shut eye," Kyle says.

"Yes, I definitely have an early morning tomorrow."

"Thank you so much for the ride home Leo."

"Of course, it was really good seeing you Kyle. I am really glad we got a chance to talk and clear the air," Leo says.

"Me too," Kyle responds.

Kyle walks Leo to the door.

"Goodnight Leo."

"Goodnight Kyle, you take care of yourself."

"You do the same, and congratulations again on your engagement."

"Thanks," Leo responds and walks down the hall.

Kyle closes the door and walks to her bed room.

"I am in desperate need of a shower, ugh," she says to herself."

She picks out some sweat pants and a tank top out of the dresser drawer and lays them on the bed. She turns the shower on and gets undressed.

"Leo is engaged…hmm, that was quick. We only stopped speaking six months ago," Kyle says to herself as the soapy hot water runs down her back and legs. After about twenty minutes, Kyle steps out of the shower, dries off, and walks to the bedroom.

She grabs a bottle of lavender scented baby oil gel and rubs it into her arms and legs before putting on her sweatpants and tank top.

She slips her feet into some soft fuzzy pink slippers and walks toward the living room where there are three huge boxes on the ground. She begins to go through some of the mail in one of the boxes. She finds four letters from Leo and one from Mike and Leslie in the large stack. She grabs the letters and walks to her bedroom. She opens the one from Mike and Leslie first. In it is a 5x7 sized picture of an olive skinned baby girl with a full head of curly jet black hair, dressed in a pink and white polka dot dress and matching head band with a bow. She has big round eyes and little pudgy cheeks. The bottom of the picture reads 'Tracie Monique McCall 7lbs 19 inches.'

"Wow, she is beautiful," Kyle says to herself, placing the photo on the night stand. She then begins to read each of Leo's letters one by one. Once she gets to the last page of the last letter, Kyle's eyes get a little misty. She shakes it off.

"No sense in stewing in your decision girl. You did what you believed was best," she says to herself.

Just then, she remembered the package that was on her desk in Paris that she had for gotten to open. She goes to the hall by the door and pulls it out of her smaller suitcase. She opens it to find a smaller white box in it. She takes it out the larger box and walks into her bedroom. She opens the box and finds a small card that reads, 'I am not giving up on you Kyle!'

Under the card is a ring box. Kyle opens it to see the engagement ring Patrick proposed with. She rolls her eyes and puts the box back together and puts in on the dresser.

She plugs in her cell phone and lays it on the nightstand. As she grabs another satin, this time pink, eye mask out of the nightstand drawer, her phone begins to buzz. The notification banner says there's a text from Leo. She gets in bed and unlocks her phone to open the message:

Leo: Kyle, it was really good seeing you. If I am being honest, seeing you has brought up feelings I thought had gone away. I really would like to see you again. I know I am engaged and this doesn't make me look like the greatest guy right now, but I cannot help what I feel. Please say we can have dinner sometime soon. Goodnight, Leo.

So What.........

Me and my best friend fight and make up three times a year......So what!!!!

This relationship was not what I thought it was gonna be......So what!!!

I am an overprotect mom ....So what!!!

I left my hometown and started all over, and I am terrified....So what!!!

I am always late and it drive my friends crazy...So what!!!

I have several friends with benefits....So what!!!

I love her and my wife....So what!!

I have a man 24 years my junior, so what!!

I may not like you like that but.... So what!!

Yes this is a wig...... So what? And What?

What is your so what?

I would love for you to post your so what tag line to your twitter or IG and Tag me @ IG: kym_thewriter Twitter: kym12871.

Made in the USA
San Bernardino, CA
03 December 2019

60834516R00202